Freddy was watching the Centerboro High School football team at practice. A bit chilly, he donned the nearest sweater (one of the players'). Summoned by the coach to hop to it, Freddy went out on the field. So splendid were his blocking and tackling that the Centerboro school board found itself hard put to find anything in the by-laws about preventing pigs from enrolling as students.

In the meantime the Bean family was being victimized by one Aaron Doty. Between helping out his best friends, the Beans, and worrying about the big game between Centerboro and Tushville, Freddy had his trotters full.

The Complete FREDDY THE PIG Series
Available or Coming Soon from the Overlook Press

FREDDY

PLAYS FOOTBALL

~.~.~.~.~.~.~.~.~.~.~.~.~.

Pretty soon he put it on to see what it was like.

FREDDY
PLAYS
FOOTBALL

by WALTER R. BROOKS

Illustrated by Kurt Wiese

If you enjoyed this book, very likely you will be interested not only in the other Freddy books published in this series, but also in joining the *Friends of Freddy,* an organization of Freddy devotees.

We will be pleased to hear from any reader about our "Freddy" publishing program. You can easily contact us by logging on the either THE OVERLOOK PRESS website, or the Freddy website.

The website addresses are as follows:
THE OVERLOOK PRESS:
www.overlookpress.com

FREDDY:
www.friendsoffreddy.org

We look forward to hearing from you soon.

First published in the United States in 2001 by
The Overlook Press, Peter Mayer Publishers, Inc.
Woodstock & New York

WOODSTOCK:
One Overlook Drive
Woodstock, NY 12498
www.overlookpress.com
[for individual orders, bulk and special sales, contact our Woodstock office]

NEW YORK:
386 West Broadway
New York, NY 10012

Library of Congress Cataloging-in-Publication Data

Brooks, Walter R., 1886-1958.
Freddy plays football / Walter R. Brooks ; illustrated by Kurt Wiese.
p. cm.
Summary: While clever Freddy the pig tries to find out if Mrs. Bean's long-lost brother is really her brother, he also attends school so that he will be eligible to play in the big football game between Centerboro and Tushville.
[1. Pigs—Fiction. 2. Football—Fiction. 3. Imposters and imposture—Fiction. 4. Humorous stories. 5. Mystery and detective stories.] I. Wiese, Kurt, 1887- ill. II. Title.
PZ7.B7994 Fre 2001 [Fic]—dc21 2001021097

Manufactured in the United States of America
ISBN 1-58567-133-9
1 3 5 7 9 8 6 4 2

FREDDY

PLAYS FOOTBALL

Chapter 1

Jinx, the black cat, was curled up in the exact center of the clean white counterpane that Mrs. Bean had just put on the spare room bed.

Jinx had no business there. He had his own bed, a soft red cushion down behind the stove that Mrs. Bean had made for him. Mrs. Bean was fond of Jinx, but she wasn't fond of having him on the beds, and she particularly didn't like him on the spare room bed. He knew that if she caught him on her own bed she would pick him up and throw him off. But if she caught him on the spare room bed she would chase him with a broom.

Now Jinx's red cushion was much more

comfortable than the bed, but there wasn't anything very exciting about taking a nap on it. In the spare room, on the other hand, you never knew when Mrs. Bean might appear in the doorway and a sweep of the broom would send you head over heels on to the floor. Like most cats, Jinx enjoyed a spice of danger, even when he was asleep.

He wasn't really asleep of course; he was just taking a cat nap. His eyes would close for a few seconds, then they would open and he would look at his reflection in the mirror over the bureau. He looked very black against the white counterpane. "My goodness," he would say, "I certainly am a darned handsome cat!" Then he would close his eyes and purr for a minute. But pretty soon his eyes would pop open again. "Yes, sir," he would say, "I certainly am distinguished looking. Elegant! That's the word —elegant!" And he would purr louder than ever.

He purred so loud that when the four mice, Eek and Quik and Eeny and Cousin Augustus, came into the room and climbed up on the windowsill behind him, he didn't hear them at all. They sat in a row and watched him admiring himself, and they poked one another and snickered until at last Eeny got to giggling so hard that he fell right off the windowsill. He only made a very small thump when he hit the carpet. But Jinx heard it, and in one bound he was off the bed and under the bureau.

The mice were delighted with this, because it isn't often that a mouse scares a cat—it's usually the other way round. They giggled harder than ever, and Eeny climbed up on the footboard of the bed and jumped down on the counterpane. "Come on, fellows," he said, "let's see how we look." So the others came over and they sat in a row with their paws on each other's shoulders and looked in the mirror.

"Boy oh boy!" said Eek. "What pretty little fellows we are, to be sure!"

"Very intellectual looking," said Quik. "And such sweet expressions!"

"It isn't just good looks," said Eeny. "We've got charm! That's the word—charm!" And they held on to one another and rocked back and forth with laughter.

"Yeah," said Cousin Augustus, "what's an old cat got that we haven't got, hey?"

"He's got claws," said Jinx, coming out from under the bureau. "Don't you know this spare room is out of bounds to animals?"

"Oh, yeah?" said Eek. "What are you doing here then?"

"I'll show you what I'm doing here," said the cat, and made a leap for the bed.

The mice scattered, hopped to the floor, and then ran up the window curtains and sat on the curtain rod. They weren't really scared, for Jinx was not only an old and trusted friend, but a good-natured cat, who could take a joke on himself without getting mad. Still, he was apt to play pretty rough and if he caught them he would tickle them until they squeaked for help.

"Come down off there!" he commanded. "Do you want me to come up after you?"

"Sure, come on up," said Eeny. He knew that Jinx couldn't climb the curtains without tearing them, and if Mrs. Bean found them torn the cat would not only get the old broom treatment, he would probably be banished from the house.

Jinx shrugged his shoulders. "Pooh," he said, "I wouldn't demean myself!" He hopped up on the bed and lay down again. "I can wait. You'll have to come down some time."

The mice giggled some more, and Quik shook his head. "Uh-uh," he said. "We like it

In one bound he was off the bed.

here. Matter of fact, we think of settling here. It's a fine location—lots of fresh air, beautiful view—except for cats, of course—'' He broke off. "Psst! Beat it, cat," he squeaked. "Mrs. Bean's coming up the back stairs!"

Jinx had heard the footsteps too. There was just a flicker of black as he disappeared through the doorway. The mice stayed where they were, for they were so close to the ceiling that they were sure of not being seen. People coming into a room seldom look above the level of their eyes.

Mrs. Bean was a plump little woman with black hair and red cheeks and snapping black eyes. She came in and looked at the bed, and she frowned. You and I wouldn't have seen anything wrong with it. The counterpane would have looked to us as smooth and white as a fresh sheet of paper. But Mrs. Bean was, I guess, one of the best housekeepers that ever lived, and she spotted right away the faint indentation where Jinx had lain, and the two or three little wrinkles his feet had made when he jumped off and on the bed. She put her hand on the indentation and felt of it. "Warm!" she said. "Drat that cat!" She smoothed out the counterpane, and then after looking under the bureau to see if Jinx was hiding there, she went back downstairs.

Now when she was coming up the back stairs, Jinx was sneaking down the front ones, and when she got back to the kitchen, there he was, snoozing peacefully on his cushion back of the stove. She looked at him hard, but he kept his eyes shut and even threw in a little snore for good measure, so that she couldn't help smiling. "Jinx, you wretch," she said, "I know you're not asleep."

Jinx gave a start and his eyes snapped open. "What—what?" he said. "Oh, it's you, ma'am. You startled me."

"I'd have startled you with a good box on the ear if I'd caught you on that spare room bed."

"The spare room bed?" he inquired innocently. "Good gracious, has someone been up there?"

"I know you won't lie to me if I ask if it was you," she said, "but you've put on such a good show that I won't ask. I'll just suggest that you'd better go without your supper tonight."

"Oh, gosh, Mrs. Bean," he protested, "I need my supper. I'm a growing cat—"

"You're growing much too smart for your own good," she said. "Now let's not have any argument. You know perfectly well you're not allowed in that room. My brother is coming to-morrow to pay us a visit, and what do you think he'd say about my housekeeping if he saw his bed all mussed up?"

"He'd better not say anything in front of me!" Jinx exclaimed.

"That's very good of you," said Mrs. Bean drily. "But, land sakes, I'm not going to stand here arguing all afternoon with a cat!" She went and opened the back door. "You go on out for a while. Go on. Scat!"

"Yes, ma'am," said Jinx meekly, and went.

He went straight across the barnyard, past the stable, where he could hear Hank, the old white horse, munching hay, and past the cow barn, where he could hear the three cows munching their cuds. Everybody seemed to be munching something. Even Charles, the rooster, and his wife, Henrietta, were walking around in front of the henhouse, picking up kernels of corn. "If I'm going to get any supper tonight," he thought, "I've got to get busy." So he walked up to the pig pen and rapped on the door.

Freddy, the pig, had learned to read and write when he was quite young. Later, he had taught most of the other animals on the Bean farm. But it wasn't much good to them at first, because there was nothing for them to read. So Freddy started a newspaper for them. It was called the Bean Home News, and it is today the only important animal newspaper in New York State. Jinx knew that Freddy was getting the next issue of the paper ready to send to the printer, so when a voice called impatiently for him to come in, he pushed open the door.

"Hi, pig!" he said breezily. "Got a spot of hot news for the old scandal sheet!"

Freddy was sitting in his old armchair before the typewriter. He swung round. "The last bit of hot news you brought in here, Jinx," he said, "was about as hot as a last week's griddle cake. About the cow that flew a plane across the continent. Not only did it happen three years ago, but a lot of your story wasn't true. She didn't fly the plane—she was just a passenger."

"So what?" said the cat. "It was a good story, wasn't it? Caused a lot of talk, and that's what makes a paper interesting. Shucks, if a story's good, it's good, no matter how old it is. Look at the one about Captain John Smith and Pocahontas. That's hundreds of years old, and it's still a good story."

"Sure, but it's not news. Look, Jinx; a news

story is a *new* story, not an old one. Suppose I printed the story about Captain John Smith. With these headlines: 'Capt. Smith to Wed. Pocahontas' Plea Wins Irate Father's Pardon For Gallant Soldier. Powhatan Sanctions Immediate Nuptials.' Why everybody'd laugh themselves sick."

"O K, O K," said Jinx. "Never mind the fancy talk. Anyhow, you've got it all wrong. Let me write your headlines, and I bet every animal on the farm would read the story. Something like this: 'Love Halts Smith Execution. Princess Perils Life to Save Lover. Today, yelling "I love him," Pocahontas, famous Indian beauty, grabbed her father's uplifted war club as he was about to sock that well known—' "

"Oh, skip it, Jinx," Freddy interrupted. "I'm busy. What's your hot news?"

"It's something pretty special," said Jinx. "If you'll invite me to supper, I'll be glad to give it to you."

"What do you want to have supper with me for?" Freddy asked.

"Well, Mrs. Bean is sort of off me today. She has some idea I've been up on the spare room bed, and—well, she isn't going to give me any."

"Ha!" said Freddy. "That's a good news

story. 'Jinx Ejected From Spare Room. No Supper, Mrs. Bean Rules.' " He turned to make a note with a pencil, but Jinx said: "Shucks, Freddy, that isn't news. I've been thrown out of that room more times than you could count. Look, do you want my news item?"

"Sure. But you know I only eat a light supper."

"The lighter the better, as long as there's plenty of it." The cat grinned. "O K, the news is that Mrs. Bean's brother is coming tomorrow for a visit."

"Didn't know she had a brother," Freddy said, and reached again for his pencil. "All right, what's the brother's name, and where does he live?"

"How should I know?" said the cat. "What's it matter?"

"Look," said Freddy patiently. "A newspaper story is no good unless it has all the facts in it. Suppose a store is robbed. You can't just say: A store on Main Street was robbed last night and some things stolen. You have to give the name of the store and the name and address of the owner, and a list of what was stolen, and the names and addresses of the robbers—"

"Suppose they didn't leave them. Suppose

they just took the things home and didn't have them sent? Oh well, maybe I can get some more facts. What time do we eat?"

"Six sharp. And remember—no facts, no food."

Two minutes later Jinx was mewing hopefully at the back door of the farmhouse. Presently the door opened. "Oh well, come in then," said Mrs. Bean.

"Look, Mrs. Bean," said the cat; "you said your brother was coming tomorrow, and I— that is, some of us thought it would be sort of nice to have a reception committee, and maybe a little speech of welcome and a bouquet of flowers or something."

"Why, Jinx," said Mrs. Bean, "that's a very nice thought. I think it would be lovely."

"Well, ma'am, the trouble is, we don't know his name or where he comes from or anything, and it's kind of hard to compose a speech unless we have—well, some facts—"

"Good land!" said Mrs. Bean. "I couldn't compose a speech if I had a bushel basket full of facts. Much less deliver it." She went over and sat down in her rocking chair.

"Well, now, it's quite a story, Jinx," she said.

"Here, hop up in my lap and I'll tell you about it.

"You see, I had an older brother, Aaron. Aaron Doty. When I was about eleven, Aaron ran away and went out west somewhere, and we lost track of him. From that day to this we've never heard a word from him, although when my father died, we tried to find him, because my father left me some money, and half of it would have belonged to Aaron. Then I got married and moved out here, and to tell you the truth I haven't thought much about him since.

"Well, sir, one day I was talking with that Mr. Boomschmidt who comes through here with his circus every year, and I told him the story and said if he ever met an Aaron Doty, to tell him to write to me. Mr. Boomschmidt travels all over the country, and I thought he just might happen to run into Aaron. And sure enough he did! And now Aaron's coming to stay with us for a while."

So Jinx thanked her and went back and told Freddy.

"Now we're getting somewhere," said the pig. "I'll just jot that down. Now this reception committee—we'll have to go through with it,

I'm afraid; but it's a good idea anyway. We'll let Charles handle it—he'll take care of the whole thing if we let him make a speech. Go over and tell him while I write this up for the paper. Then we'll have supper."

Chapter 2

Just before sunrise the next morning Charles, the rooster, came sleepily out of the henhouse door. He flew up on a fencepost and crowed. For a minute nothing happened. Then something red and white appeared in the Beans' bedroom window, and Charles knew that it was Mr. Bean's nightcap, and that the farmer was looking out to see what the weather was. And at the same time the bright gold edge of the sun appeared above the eastern horizon.

Charles crowed some more, rather impatiently. He had got the Beans up, and the cows, too—they were coming out of the barn door. But even now the sun was barely peeking over the edge of the world, like a lazy boy who peeks out from the bedclothes and has to be called a dozen times before he will get up. This annoyed Charles. The sun ought to jump right up into the sky at the first crow. A good many roosters feel the same way.

Pretty soon the little revolving door in the henhouse began to go round and round as, one by one, Charles' seventeen daughters came running out. They were going up the lane to pick wildflowers for the bouquet. Charles glared crossly at the sun. "I suppose I'd better stay here a while," he thought. "Just in case the lazy thing tries to crawl back into bed again. Ha, there's Freddy. He's another lazy one."

The pig came down to the fence, rubbing his eyes. "Morning, Charles. Got your speech of welcome ready, I suppose?"

"Oh, I haven't prepared anything," Charles said. "I prefer to leave what I say to the inspiration of the moment. Sounds more sincere, I always think. Excuse me a second." He crowed again, then said: "It'll be the usual thing. Light and graceful, rather flowery, with a humorous anecdote or two."

"Well, make it short," said Freddy.

"I think I'm quite capable of handling a few informal remarks without any instructions from you," Charles said huffily.

"Sure you are. Just see that it *is* a few. I don't want this Mr. Doty to fall flat on his face with exhaustion before you finish."

Charles hopped down from the post and strutted off angrily, and Freddy walked down to the old elm that stood beside the house and rapped on the trunk. "Hi, Freddy," said a small sleepy voice from high up among the branches.

"Morning, J.J.," said Freddy. "I've got everything ready. Drop around when you've had breakfast."

"I'm ready now," said the voice. "I'll have breakfast at Miss McMinnickle's on the way to town. She's been digging in her garden and I expect she's turned up some nice fat worms."

Mr. J. J. Pomeroy flew down and lit on a branch above Freddy's head. He was a plump and handsome robin, and the little spectacles which he wore for his nearsightedness glittered in the early sun. Every week, when Freddy had typed out all the stuff for the next issue of the

Bean Home News, Mr. Pomeroy flew it down to the printer in Centerboro.

Freddy shuddered at the thought of angleworms for breakfast, and he shuddered again when Mr. Pomeroy turned and called up to his wife that he would bring back a few for the children.

"Those little green ones, dear," Mr. Pomeroy called back. "The children are so fond of them."

Freddy hurried back to the pig pen and tied up the roll of typewritten sheets with string, and Mr. Pomeroy picked it up by the loop in the string and flew off to Centerboro. And the pig went back into his study and sat down in his big chair and put his feet up on the typewriter and took a little nap.

Along about half past ten all the animals on the Bean farm suddenly stopped whatever they were doing and lifted their heads and listened. First they thought Mrs. Bean had fallen down the back stairs with her arms full of tin pans. But the sound kept on growing louder and louder, with sort of a sputtering under the tin pan clatter, and then down the road came a little rusty old car, and as everyone rushed out into the barnyard, it roared in the gate, gave a couple of extra loud bangs, and stopped with a jerk by the back door. And with a final bang a little man was blown right out of it and up the steps, and knocked on the door.

He was a small wiry man in rather shabby clothes, and as he knocked, he shouted: "Hey, Martha! Martha Doty—I mean Bean! It's me —it's your long-lost brother Aaron." And when Mrs. Bean came to the door he seized her and hugged her, and then held her off with his hands on her shoulders. "Well, well, well!" he exclaimed. "The same old Martha! Yessir, old Martha! well, well, well!"

"Old, your grandmother!" said Mrs. Bean. "I'm five years younger than you are, Aaron. If you *are* Aaron!" She pushed him away and looked at him. "I'd certainly never have known you."

"Well, well, I'm Aaron all right," he said. "And I'd certainly 'a' known you. Look of father you've got—round the eyes. Not the beard, of course. Remember that beard, how it tickled when he kissed you goodnight? And how he used to put it in curl papers at night?"

"I guess you're Aaron all right," she said.

Then she called to Mr. Bean, who was coming across from the barn. "Mr. B! Brother Aaron's here at last!"

"Well, I kinda thought I heard somebody tiptoein' in the gate," said Mr. Bean. "How are you, Aaron?"

Mr. Doty seized Mr. Bean's hand. "So this is William, eh? Well, well, well!"

"He hasn't got much of a vocabulary," said Jinx, who was sitting with the mice in the window.

"He's got a good big trunk there in the back seat though," said Eeny. "Must be planning on a long visit."

"My land, Aaron," said Mrs. Bean, "you must be about tuckered out, driving so far. Come in and sit down. —Or, no, I guess we'll have to wait a minute—the animals want to welcome you," she said, as Charles, leading his entire family, and followed by the three cows and Freddy and Hank and the two dogs, Robert and Georgie, and Bill, the goat, strutted up to the back porch.

Mr. Doty turned to face them. "So these are the talking animals old Boomschmidt told me about! Well, well, well! Howdy, animals."

Charles flew up on to the porch. "Mr. Aaron

Doty, sir," he said pompously, "as chairman of the reception committee, and as spokesman for the animals here assembled, I wish first to present you with this inexpensive, yet heartfelt token of our affectionate friendship." He motioned with a claw to Georgie, who walked unsteadily up the steps on his hind legs with an enormous bouquet of daisies and black-eyed Susans, and presented them to the visitor.

"Well, well, well!" said Mr. Doty. "Flowers and friendship, eh? Flowers I ain't got much use for. Hundreds here, and only one buttonhole to put 'em in. But friendship—yes; friendship I go for. Yes, sir, I do."

"Also and furthermore," Charles continued, "on behalf of all the livestock here represented, on behalf of every animal, bird and insect; on behalf of every creature that walks, flies, hops, creeps, crawls or slithers over the fields of Bean; on behalf of the inhabitants of every barn, nest, den, hole, burrow or coop on these premises, I welcome you, and extend the warm claw of—"

At this point the animals all began to cheer. Charles looked annoyed, but when the cheering died down, he resumed. "I extend the warm claw—" Again the cheering interrupted him.

Four times he tried angrily to go on, but each

time cheers drowned him out. And at last Mrs. Bean held up her hand for silence. "Come, come, animals," she said. "Let Charles finish."

But Charles was mad. He hopped down from the porch. "Let 'em make their own speech—they're so darn smart!" he said, and stalked off towards the henhouse. So then after Mr. Doty had shaken hands with all the animals and thanked them he and the Beans went into the house.

Freddy walked back to the cow barn with Mrs. Wiggins. Although a cow, and therefore a pretty slow thinker, Mrs. Wiggins had a lot of what is commonly called horse sense, although cows have a good deal more than horses —or indeed than some people; and Freddy valued her opinion highly. As a partner in his detective business she had solved some of his most puzzling cases. Now he said: "Charles didn't get that warm claw extended very far, did he?"

"I've been puzzling over that," said the cow. "Wish I'd heard the rest of it. Whose claw was he talking about?"

"Oh, that was just Charles' highfalutin way of saying 'Welcome.' He was going to extend the claw of fellowship, or friendship, or some-

Georgie . . . presented them to the visitor.

thing." Freddy thought for a minute. "You know, there's something about that Doty I don't like."

"Good land," said Mrs. Wiggins, "that's nothing against him. I guess there's something about everybody on this farm you and I don't like. Even our best friends. But if they're friends, you just have to shut your eyes to such things. Usually they aren't very important."

"Goodness!" said Freddy. "Are there many things about me you don't like, Mrs. Wiggins?"

"Well," said the cow, "you don't think you're perfect, do you?"

"No. I wouldn't claim that."

"I guess that's your answer, then," she said.

After a minute Freddy said: "Well, I'm glad you like me, anyway. And I guess I'd better work a little harder at correcting my faults. What would you say was my worst one?"

The cow shook her head. "Let's stay friends, and you figure that out for yourself."

"H'm," said Freddy. And after a minute: "Look, Mrs. W., did you notice that big trunk of Mr. Doty's, in the back of his car? It has got initials painted on the end of it. But they aren't his initials, which would be A. D. Don't you think that's funny?"

"Don't know as I do," said the cow. "That boy that comes out here from Centerboro to see you all the time—Jackson, Jabez—"

"Jason Brewer," said Freddy.

"Yes. Well, he has the initials C.H.S. on his sweater. But they aren't his initials."

"Oh, that stands for Centerboro High School," Freddy said. "He played on their football team last year."

"So that's it!" said Mrs. Wiggins. "Well, maybe Mr. Doty played on some team. Maybe it stands for the Canastota Buffaloes, or the Catskill Bullfrogs. Did you ever do that game, Freddy, where you take somebody's initials and make up a sentence describing them? Like with you, F.B. would be 'fairly bright,' or 'fat banker'—"

"Or 'first-class brains,'" said Freddy. "Yeah, somebody made up one last year when the Centerboro team lost its eighth consecutive game against Tushville. They said C.H.S. meant 'Can't Hope to Score.' It was about right, too—they got licked 60-0."

Mrs. Wiggins wasn't interested in football. "Well," she said, "it's kind of funny about Mr. Doty. If he went away from Centerboro thirty years ago, and never wrote to his family or anything, he couldn't have cared much about 'em. Why come back now?"

"I can make a good guess," said Freddy. "He looks shabby, and that old car of his—golly, I bet if you gave it a good wash there wouldn't be anything left but the wheels. He's broke, and he probably figures he can get three free meals a day as long as Mrs. Bean will let him stay."

"And didn't Mrs. Bean tell Jinx that there was some money their father left them?"

"That's right," said Freddy. "Half the money she got from her father was to go to him. Wouldn't you think he'd have claimed it before this?"

"Maybe he didn't know about it. But I wonder how Mr. Boomschmidt happened to find him?"

They heard something about that when Jinx came out to the barn a little later. "Boy, that Brother Aaron is quite a card!" said the cat. "Talk about adventures! — he's been about everywhere except to the moon, and he claims he's going there in a rocket next spring. Cousin Augustus got so excited listening to his stories that he's got the hiccups again."

"How'd he find out where Mrs. Bean lives?" Freddy asked.

"Why, ever since she asked Mr. Boom-schmidt to let her know if he ever met anybody named Aaron Doty, there's been a sign posted in the circus entrance. 'Aaron Doty will learn something to his advantage if he will communicate with the management'—something like that. So one day, along comes Aaron, looking for a circus job, and sees the sign, and he goes in and says to old Boom: 'What's this about Aaron Doty?' 'His sister in Centerboro is trying to find him,' says Boom. 'Are you him?' 'Sure,' says Aaron, 'I'm her long-lost brother. Where does she live at?' So Boom tells him and he jumps in that bang-buggy of his and comes along."

Mrs. Wiggins sighed. "How romantic!" she said. "A brother she hasn't seen in thirty years!"

"I guess maybe it doesn't seem very romantic to the Beans," said Freddy. "A brother they've got to hand over a lot of cash to."

Chapter 3

In a short time Mr. Doty was very popular with the animals on the Bean farm. The stories of his adventures were endless, and he seemed to like nothing better than to tell them to anybody who would listen. He spent most of his time sitting on the back porch, surrounded by a crowd of pop-eyed animals, gasping at the tale of some hair-raising exploit.

Charles was the only one that held back. His crowing, which was a signal for everybody on the farm to get up in the morning, had no effect on Mr. Doty, who simply pulled the covers over his head and went on sleeping. Sometimes it was nearly eleven before he came downstairs. This was a challenge to Charles. On the third morning he flew right up on the windowsill of the spare room and crowed as loud as he could. Mr. Doty got up all right. He got up and threw a shoe at Charles, knocked him off the sill, and badly bent one of his longest tailfeathers. Charles was pretty mad.

One hot afternoon, Jason Brewer walked out from Centerboro to see Freddy. The pig was up by the back porch, listening with some of the other animals to Mr. Doty's account of how he had once fought an Indian chief with bowie knives for the leadership of a tribe of Apaches. Mr. Doty broke off as the boy approached.

"Well, well," he said, "visitors!"

"Hello, Jason," said Freddy. "Come over and meet Mr. Doty." And when the two had shaken hands: "Did you come up to go swimming in the duck pond?"

"I thought maybe we could," said Jason. "But if you're too busy—"

"Swimmer, are you?" Mr. Doty said. "Well,

well, I used to do a little in that line, 'deed I did. Was on the Olympic team in—twenty-one, was it? I forget the year. Did I ever tell you, Freddy, how I once swam Lake Ontario?"

"Why don't you go up with us, Mr. Doty?" Freddy asked, and Jason said: "Oh, would you? You could teach us some things."

"Well, well, I could at that," said Mr. Doty. "But some other time. A bathing suit I haven't got."

Mrs. Bean, who was working near the kitchen window, put her head out. "I've got just the thing, Aaron; you wait." She disappeared and came out presently with a brown paper package. "Mr. Bean bought this," she said as she unwrapped it, "when we went to Niagara Falls on our wedding trip. He had some idea that he could go swimming there, I guess. But when he saw the falls he changed his mind." She drew out the suit and handed it to her brother.

Mr. Doty held it up and the animals giggled, for it was the kind that used to be worn fifty years ago—red and white striped, with sleeves that came below the elbow, and legs that flapped loosely around the shins.

"Well, well," said Mr. Doty, "so old William

wore this, did he? Quite a figure he must have cut. Too small for me."

"Nonsense!" said Mrs. Bean. "It'll fit fine. You go along and have your swim."

"I don't believe I'd better go today," said Mr. Doty. "My shoulder's been kind of bothering me—it's the old wound I got in the Spanish-American War—when we charged up San Juan Hill—"

"You must have charged up it in your baby carriage then," said Mrs. Bean sharply, "for you were only two when that war started."

Mr. Doty looked puzzled. "Well, well, is that so? I guess you're right, Martha. I been in so many wars I get 'em sort of mixed up. Well, it don't signify. The wound's there, and I ought to favor it. Wouldn't do to go in the cold water."

Just then Mr. Bean came around the corner of the house. "Hey, Aaron," he said, "want to give me a hand getting that old maple by the barn down? If we don't, the next good blow'll topple it right over on the roof."

Mr. Doty hesitated for a long minute, looking at the crosscut saw that Mr. Bean was carrying. Then he said: "Why, William, I just this minute promised Freddy I'd go up and teach him some fancy diving. How about tomorrow?"

Mr. Bean just shrugged his shoulders and went off towards the barn.

"You go help him if you want to," said Freddy.

"No, no," said Mr. Doty. "Not when I've given my word to you. No, sir; keep your word, no matter what it costs you—that's my motto."

"But you hadn't given your word yet," said Jason.

"Well, well, well; an argument, hey?" said Mr. Doty. "Why of course I hadn't *said* I'd go, right out. But I'd said so in my *mind*. I'd made up my mind, and that's the same as a promise, isn't it?"

Freddy would have liked to argue the point a little longer, but Mr. Doty got up, and with the striped bathing suit slung over his shoulder, walked across the barnyard. "Come along," he said; and when they started after him: "Did I ever teach you the Ogallala warwhoop, Freddy? It's a pretty ferocious sound. Makes your blood run cold when you're camping alone on the prairie and you hear—this!" And he took a deep breath and then let out a long high screech. "Come on—try it! That's the stuff, Freddy. Give it all you've got, Mrs. Wiggins—

we'll make a warrior out of you yet." And then as they all began imitating the screech he had given, Mr. Doty waved the bathing suit around his head and started running. "Come on!" he shouted. "We're a band of Ogallala Sioux, and we're going up to set fire to the duck pond and scalp the ducks!" And the boy and the animals pounded after him, yelling at the top of their lungs.

Alice and Emma, the two ducks, were sitting on the pond, entertaining a caller. The pond was really their parlor and dining room combined; the parlor was upstairs—that is, it was the surface of the pond; and the dining room was downstairs—the rich layer of mud on the pond's bottom, where they hunted for things to eat. They were proud of their parlor, because like all ducks they looked their best on the water, where they swam easily and gracefully. On land, their movements were neither easy nor graceful; they waddled; and even some of the best-mannered animals on the farm could not help snickering when they saw the two out for a walk.

But there were very few callers whom the ducks could entertain in their parlor. The animals usually sat on the bank, and if the ducks invited them in they always wanted to swim and splash about, which is not parlor manners and makes polite conversation impossible. But today's caller was quite at home in the water. He was Theodore, a frog from the pool up in the woods, and he floated between Alice and Emma, with just his nose and his goggle eyes sticking out, and exchanged small talk about the weather and the local gossip.

A third duck, Uncle Wesley, had not joined his nieces in the parlor. He was sitting under the shade of a burdock leaf on the bank, muttering grumpily to himself. "I have never associated with frogs," he grumbled, "and I don't intend to begin now. Horrid clammy bug-eyed creatures!"

Alice and Emma were very much embarrassed by Uncle Wesley's conduct. They tried to keep between him and Theodore, and they both chattered at a great rate so that the frog wouldn't hear their uncle's remarks. Of course Theodore did hear, but he was too polite to show it.

Emma was just remarking that she thought we were going to have an early fall, when Alice said: "Sister, what's that?"

It was of course the yelling of the Ogallala

Indians led by Mr. Doty, and as it approached I guess it was as frightening to ducks as to any camper on the lone prairie. Alice and Emma, quacking excitedly, spread their wings and skittered across the water for the shelter of the reeds at one end of the pond; and Theodore, after listening for a moment, dove down into the mud in the ducks' dining room. Uncle Wesley, peering out from under his burdock leaf, saw what he thought was an armed mob charging up the slope, brandishing a red flag. They were so close that he knew it was safer to stay where he was. He crouched down closer to the ground and put his head under his wing and trembled.

The Indians reached the pond and threw themselves down in the grass to get their breath. Then Mr. Doty went off with Jason to put on their trunks and bathing suit. The ducks heard laughter, and familiar voices, and came gliding out from among the reeds, feeling rather foolish, and Theodore, coming up presently for air, also heard them and hopped up on the bank. But Uncle Wesley, with his head under his wing, didn't hear anything. He stayed where he was.

"Well," said Freddy, "what are we waiting

for?" And he walked out to the end of the springboard that Mr. Bean had put up for the animals, and jumped in. The boy and the other animals followed, until at last everybody was in but Mr. Doty.

"Come on," said Freddy; "aren't you going to show us some dives?"

Mr. Doty sat down on the bank and put his left big toe in the water, then drew it back with a shiver. "Fancy diving I never liked much," he remarked. "Always seems too much like showing off. Anyway, my specialty was swimming races."

"What stroke do you use?" Jason asked. "Show us."

Mr. Doty shook his head. "This pool is hardly big enough for a demonstration. Terrific speed I work up—two strokes, and my head would hit the other bank."

"You couldn't work up much speed in two strokes," said Jason.

"Ha, you don't know me! No, you go ahead and enjoy yourselves. I'll get in later."

Alice and Emma were keeping off at a safe distance from the others. "I suppose that bathing suit of Mr. Doty's is the latest thing," Alice said, "but I must say it isn't very becoming."

"It's in very bad taste, if you ask me," said Emma. "So conspicuous with those bright stripes."

Theodore's head popped up between them. "What'll you bet I can't get old Dud-dud, I mean Doty into the water?" he said. Theodore always stammered a good deal, though he really didn't have to. He said he'd started doing it because when anybody asked him a question it gave him a little extra time to think up a good answer. And now he did it without thinking.

"We do not approve of betting," said Alice primly.

"Neither do I," said the frog, "unless I'm sure I can win." He winked one bulging eye at them and disappeared.

A minute later he crawled out on the bank and in two long jumps he was around behind Mr. Doty, who had lighted a cigar and was standing at the edge of the water, shouting advice and encouragement to Freddy. Then he gathered himself together and with one long spring landed square and clammy on the back of the man's neck.

Mr. Doty threw up his arms, his cigar flew out of his mouth, and with a warwhoop that would have scared any number of Ogallala Indians, he lost his balance and plunged after the cigar. Little bits of the uncompleted warwhoop came up in a string of bubbles.

Fortunately the water was not deep on that side. Mr. Doty reappeared almost immediately. As soon as he stopped sputtering, Mrs. Wiggins said: "That was a real pretty dive, Mr. Doty. And quick! My land, when you dropped your cigar, it had hardly left your mouth when you were right after it."

"Don't believe in wasting things," he said, and started to climb up on the bank.

"Aren't you going to stay in and show us some stunts?" Bill asked.

"Well, well, I'd like to. But the water's pretty cold today and the trouble is, I'm subject to cramps."

All this time Uncle Wesley had been cowering under his burdock leaf with his head tucked tightly under his wing, and he hadn't heard much of what went on. But he did hear Mr. Doty's yell. He took his head out, and there in front of him was a piratical looking stranger climbing up out of the water and apparently coming straight for him. Uncle Wesley wasn't very brave, but even a cornered duck will fight, and he felt that he was cornered. He flew up

He flew up and grabbed Mr. Doty's nose.

and grabbed Mr. Doty's nose with his strong yellow bill and twisted.

Again Mr. Doty gave the warwhoop and fell into the water—backwards this time. And again the end of the yell came up in bubbles, while Uncle Wesley fluttered free and, half flying and half swimming, made for the reeds.

Mrs. Wiggins was all admiration. "You did it again!" she exclaimed. "And backwards this time! That was wonderful!"

But Mr. Doty was mad. He scrambled ashore and picked up a stone and threw it at Uncle Wesley. His aim was poor and he barely missed Emma.

"Hey, take it easy," said Freddy. "Wes didn't mean any harm. You scared him."

"Is that so!" Mr. Doty gave Freddy a mean look. "Well, I'll wring his neck if I ever get hold of him." And he picked up another stone and threw it. This time it didn't come within yards of the ducks.

Freddy looked at Mrs. Wiggins, and then at Bill and Robert and Georgie, and they all got up and went over and stood in a ring around Mr. Doty. Jason came along too. They didn't look threatening or anything—they just stood and looked at him. And Mr. Doty, who was stooping for another stone, straightened up and gave an uneasy laugh. "Well, well, well," he said; "mad at me, are you? Why I wouldn't hurt him. Ducks I wouldn't attack. Lions and rhinoceroses, yes—done it many times. But ducks, no. Just wanted to scare him a little. I didn't try to hit him; you saw yourselves how the stones didn't come anywhere near him."

"Maybe you aren't a very good shot," said Georgie.

"Well, well, so that's what you think, eh? Let me tell you, I hit what I aim at. Why, when I was pitching for the Cards there's game after game I've struck out ten, fifteen, twenty men."

"Yeah?" said Georgie. "Let's see you hit that fence post over there."

Mr. Doty swung his right arm around a couple of times. "No," he said. "I'd better not. It's a long time since I pitched a game and my ligaments ain't real tight. Might stretch one, and then I'd be laid up good. Guess I better get this wet bathing suit off," and he went back to where he had left his clothes.

Pretty soon they started home. Freddy looked at Jason's sweater. "What have you done with the C.H.S. you used to have on that sweater?" he asked.

"I ripped it off," said the boy. "I guess I just couldn't take the kidding. You know what everybody says it means: Can't Hope to Score; Creep, Hobble and Stumble. They make up a new one every day. I don't think we'll have any team this year; I don't think anybody'll come out for it."

"Well," said Freddy, "I don't think you ought to be ashamed of being on a team just because it loses. I saw your second game with Tushville last year. You put up a good fight, but they were just too heavy."

"Quite a football player myself I used to be," put in Mr. Doty. "Never forget the game we played against Notre Dame. Made three of the four touchdowns myself. The last one, I wasn't only carrying the ball, I was carrying their big left guard, too—Winooski, his name was. He'd tried to tackle me, ye see, and I couldn't shake him off, so I just picked him up and tucked him under my other arm and carried him over the line."

Freddy had become convinced by this time that Mr. Doty's stories of his exploits were all lies. They were rather harmless lies, because Mr. Doty evidently didn't expect anybody to believe them. Nobody, for instance, could run with a two hundred pound football player under one arm. Freddy thought Mr. Doty just told them for fun. He said so to Mrs. Wiggins when they got back home.

Mrs. Wiggins didn't agree. "He wouldn't tell those stories to the Beans," she said. "No, sir, he thinks animals are stupid. Dumb animals—that's what most people call us. He thinks we'll believe anything."

"I sort of like him, though," said Freddy.

"Land sakes," said the cow, "I don't object to a liar, as such. He's a lot of fun, too. Only I wouldn't trust him much. He's using lies every day, and if he got mad at you, he'd pick up the handiest thing to get even with. And what has he always got handy?—a good fat lie."

When Jason started home, Freddy walked down to the gate with him. "I think you ought to sew those letters back on your sweater," said the pig. "You played the game hard; you've nothing to be ashamed of."

"I'm not ashamed really," said Jason. "The reason Tushville has piled up such big scores is that they've got a lot of ringers on their team. There's four of those boys in the last game that must be twenty years old; I bet they don't even go to school."

"Well, can't you do anything about it?"

"I don't see how. We tried to get Mr. Gridley, our principal, to do something, but he doesn't like football and he wouldn't. He thinks we ought not to have a team anyway. Can't you think of something, Freddy?"

"Why, sure," said Freddy. "Sure. I've got several ideas already. H'm, let me see . . . Give me a day or two to mull it over, Jason. So long now."

Freddy's conscience bothered him as he walked back to the pig pen. He'd said that he had several ideas. That was true enough. But they weren't very good ideas. "I suppose it's an idea to put a lot of lions and tigers into football suits and have them play on the Centerboro team. And it's an idea to shoot all the Tushville team. But they're neither of them really ideas because they couldn't be used. I guess I'll have to make good on this. I guess I'll really have to do a little mulling, whatever that is. I don't want to get like Mr. Doty."

Chapter 4

Mr. and Mrs. Webb were two spiders who had been happily married for many years. They had led a quiet life on the farm, until the winter when the Bean animals had gone to Florida. The Webbs had gone along. The trip, during most of which they had ridden on Mrs. Wiggins' head, had been a wonderful experience for them, and had changed their whole lives. For it had given them a desire to travel.

Now spiders are not generally great travelers. Of course they have plenty of legs, but their legs are too short. For Mr. Webb to go from the barn up to the duck pond would be as hard and dangerous as for you to travel through fifty miles of a tropical jungle, since grass is tough going for anything as small as a spider. But the Webbs had worked it out. They hitch-hiked.

They did it this way. Let's say they wanted to go over to Tushville, about ten miles beyond Centerboro. It was easy enough to get to Centerboro. Freddy went down at least once a week, and they could get a ride on him. Or if they couldn't ride any other way, they'd wait until Mr. Bean hitched Hank up to the buggy, and then they would hop on to Mr. Bean and climb up and hide under his coat collar. They could have ridden on Hank, of course, but Hank didn't like it—he said they tickled.

Then when Mr. Bean stopped in Centerboro they would wait in the buggy until they spotted a car which seemed to be headed in the right direction, and they would hop down and get aboard it. Sometimes, of course, they would end up in South Pharisee or Pocanaxon, and once they got carried clear to Albany without a chance to get down. But they didn't care. It was all interesting, and they stayed a couple of days and saw the sights and even had dinner with the Governor—at least they sat on his collar during the meal.

Mrs. Webb enjoyed going to weddings and crying a little when the bride walked up the aisle, and Mr. Webb liked them too, because he could look at the presents and figure out what they cost. So one day several months before Mr. Doty's arrival at the farm, they were returning from Utica, where they had attended a large wedding. The young man with whom they had ridden from Centerboro had come alone, but on the return trip a young lady rode with him. They had expected that he would stop in Centerboro, but he drove right on through, and they learned from the conversation that he was going to Syracuse.

The Webbs didn't mind. "We haven't been in Syracuse in some time," said Mr. Webb. "Perhaps if we are smart we can take in a movie before we go home."

But the car didn't go into the city, it turned out towards the airport. The young man turned to his companion. "Well," he said, "there's your plane. They'll be loading in a few minutes. Have a good time in Hollywood."

"Good land!" said Mrs. Webb. "We'd better jump!"

The spiders had been riding under a bow of ribbon on the front of the young lady's hat.

For a traveling spider, no safer or more comfortable spot can be found than a lady's hat. It was the Pullman car of spider travel, Mr. Webb said. For women are careful of their hats; they never throw them around or put them where they'll be sat on, as men do; and there are usually flowers or feathers to hide under.

Mr. Webb got ready to jump to the young man's shoulder, then he hesitated. "We haven't ever flown, mother," he said thoughtfully.

"Good grief!" Mrs. Webb exclaimed. "You don't mean you'd trust yourself to one of those flimsy contraptions?"

"Hollywood's quite a place, they tell me," Mr. Webb continued.

Mrs. Webb laughed. "Well, I must say, Webb, you get some very unspiderlike ideas. But good land, there's nothing that calls us home. Though how you ever expect to get back—"

"Oh, we'll get back somehow," said her husband.

So that was how the Webbs went to Hollywood. And they really had a wonderful time. They met several prominent West Coast spiders, and were royally entertained, and visited a number of studios, and their adventures would fill a book. They even got into the pictures, although you can't see them unless you know just where to look. Except in one called *The Masked Bandit*. In that one, the hero is sound asleep in bed, and the bandits are creeping up to break into the cabin. Mr. Webb was on the ceiling of the cabin when they were shooting that scene, and he got so worried that the hero wouldn't wake up in time, that he let himself down on a long strand and landed on the man's nose. The hero sneezed and woke up in time. Of course the director didn't plan it that way, but it was so exciting that he said he'd keep the scene the way it was. And I guess he would have made a big fuss over Mr. Webb, and maybe even given him a part in the next picture, but Mr. Webb couldn't be found. He had been blown on to the floor by the hero's sneeze and quite badly bruised, but he managed to crawl down a knothole so that he wouldn't be stepped on, and Mrs. Webb took care of him there for two or three days until he could walk without limping. After that she wouldn't let him visit the studios any more, and a few days later they started east.

It took them nearly two months to hitch-hike home. They didn't have much luck with planes. They only flew once—from Denver to Chicago; the rest of the way they traveled mostly by car. Often the car they were riding in would turn off in the wrong direction and carry them miles out of their way. But they were in no hurry. Sometimes when they found themselves in a quiet spot where there were plenty of flies, they would spin a web and rest a few days. They really had a wonderful trip.

They got back to Centerboro about the middle of September. They came in on a milk truck, and when it stopped at the filling station for gas, they hopped down, climbed to the top of the gas pump, and waited. Several cars stopped for gas, but they were going in the wrong direction. But at last one pulled in that was headed for the road that led past the Bean farm. It was a shaky old rattletrap and the engine seemed to be trying to smash its way out from under the hood.

"Well," said Mr. Webb, "it isn't the kind of shiny powerful car us big movie actors are accustomed to riding in, mother, and that's a fact. But I guess it's all there is. Come along."

So they climbed into the car. The driver was a small, shabby man, and when he had bought two gallons of gas he didn't drive on imme-

The hero sneezed and woke up.

diately, he pulled off to one side. Pretty soon another car drew up behind him and a man got out and came up and said: "Well, how's it going?"

The Webbs looked at each other. They didn't know that the first man was Mr. Doty, because they had never seen or heard of him. But they knew the other man all right. He was Mr. Herbert Garble, who had once given the Bean animals a good deal of trouble, and had even tried to kidnap and sell Freddy.

"Going fine," said Mr. Doty. "Only how's about slipping your old pal Doty a little more folding money? I'm running short."

Mr. Garble frowned. "I've already advanced your expenses getting here. I told you I wasn't going to keep shelling out after you got settled in. Anyway, you're taking too long."

"You got to go slow in these things. Money I can't start talking about—not till they bring it up themselves. They'll get suspicious."

"Yeah?" said Mr. Garble. "Well, you want to look out for that pig. He's a detective, and I'm telling you—he's good."

"Well, well, well," said Mr. Doty, "just because those animals can talk, you think they're smart, huh? Well, they're animals, ain't they?

If they were smart, they wouldn't be animals, would they?"

"I don't know how you figure that out."

"Never mind how I figure it. I'm telling you. Heck, I kid 'em along and they think I'm wonderful."

"Well, I admit that's not too smart of them," Mr. Garble said.

"Well, well; *ve-ry* funny!" said Mr. Doty. "I tell you I got 'em all eating right out of my hand. And now how about that money?"

Mr. Garble pulled a couple of bills out and handed them over. "I hope you know what you're doing," he said. "And while those animals are eating out of your hand, keep an eye on your fingers. You might lose one or two." He turned away. "Meet me here again Friday. So long."

As they clattered out of town the Webbs sat on Mr. Doty's coat collar and talked over what they had heard. They couldn't make much sense out of it. "Well, mother," Mr. Webb said at last, "whatever this Doty is plotting, I don't think he'll get very far with it. Not if he figures Freddy for stupid. We'd better tell Freddy all this right away." He looked out at the landscape, familiar now that they were nearing

home. "My, my!" he said. "Won't it be wonderful to get back and see everybody again!
Aren't you excited, mother?"

She said: "I certainly am. I've been trying
to think of that song Freddy made up—you
know, about getting back home." She began
to hum it.

"You've got a real nice voice, mother," said
Mr. Webb. "I like to hear you sing." And indeed her voice was very sweet, though of course
pretty small, and about two octaves higher than
a mosquito's.

"Sing with me, Webb," she said. "You used
to have a fine rich tenor."

So Mr. Webb joined in. This is what they
sang:

Oh, a life of adventure is gay and free,
  And danger has its thrill;
And no spider of spirit will bound his life
  By the web on the windowsill.

    Yet many a wandering spider sighs
    For the pleasant tang of the home-grown
      flies.

But one tires at last of wandering
  As summer fades to fall.

And the year is old, and the wind grows cold,
And the flies are few and small.

> *Then each spider knows that, by Jan. or*
> *Feb.,*
> *He'll be better off in the old home web.*

Mr. Webb had changed the song a good deal
so it would be about spiders. But it sounded
quite nice, though naturally nobody heard it.
And pretty soon their car drove in the Bean
gate, stopped with a final bang, and Mr. Doty
hopped out.

The Webbs of course hopped out with him,
but as he went in the back door they dropped
off and went up to Jinx, who was asleep in the
sunshine, and swung on his whiskers until he
woke up.

"Well, where did you two come from?" the
cat demanded. "Golly, this calls for a celebra-
tion. Where've you been all summer—on one
of those trips of yours? You might have dropped
us a postcard."

"Look, Jinx," said Mr. Webb, "we've got
some important news. About this Mr. Doty we
drove home with. Who is he anyway?"

"That's right," said the cat, "you don't know
about him. Why, he's Mrs. Bean's brother. If

you've got news about him, let's go up to the pig pen and talk to the big editor. If you aren't too proud to travel by cat, after riding in that high-class thunder-buggy of Doty's."

Freddy and Jinx were both puzzled by what the Webbs had to tell. "Let me see, now," said the pig, frowning importantly and putting on his Great Detective expression and no non-sense about it either, please! "Doty claims to have come straight on here from the west, where he's been all these years. How is it he knows Garble, then? And why is Garble giving him money? And what did Garble mean—"

"Hey, look, pig," said Jinx impatiently, "those are questions we're asking *you.* What's the sense of asking them back to us again?"

"Quiet, *please!*" said Freddy, closing his eyes and putting one fore trotter to his brow. "In detective work you know very well that I am competent and reliable. Mr. Garble, although an old enemy of mine, has himself admitted it. Now in considering a case, my method is to ask all possible questions about it, and then to find a theory that will answer them all. Then the case is solved . . ."

"O K, O K," said Jinx, winking at the Webbs. "Give with the theory, master mind."

"Well," said Freddy, "you remember, Jinx, that Mrs. Bean told you that they tried for a long time to find her brother, because half the money her father left really belonged to him."

"You mean Doty's here for the money, and he's going to split it with Garble?"

"Please let me continue," said Freddy severely. "Doty is certainly here for the money. But why should he split with Garble? Have you ever asked yourself—is Doty Doty?"

"I certainly have not!" said Jinx. "You trying to be funny?"

"I'm trying to show you that Mr. Doty isn't what he says he is. I don't think he's Mrs. Bean's brother at all. I think he's somebody that Garble got to come here and pass himself off as Aaron Doty, in order to get the real Doty's money."

"But Mrs. Bean says he's her brother," said Mr. Webb. "Didn't she recognize him?"

"How could she recognize him when she hasn't seen him since she was a little girl? He said he was her brother, and he told her a few things about when she was little that probably Mr. Garble had found out for him. So she believed him. It's pretty easy to believe something when you want to a lot."

" 'Tisn't easy for me to believe that you owe me a lot of money," said Jinx, "though I sure want to."

"But what can we do about it?" Mrs. Webb asked.

"If there was time," said Freddy, "we ought to do some detective work on Doty—find out who he really is. But Mrs. Bean may turn over the money to him any day, and as soon as she does he'll be off over the hills, and our chance is gone."

"She's going to give him the money," said Jinx. "They were all talking about it the other night. Doty said there wasn't any hurry, but Mrs. Bean said: 'Yes, there is, too! That money belongs to you, Aaron, and you're going to have it.' But later that night, after Doty had gone to bed, the Beans were talking, and I guess they're going to have a hard time raising the money. They were thinking of selling something—I couldn't make out whether it was land, or some of the animals."

"My goodness," said Freddy, "that would probably be the cows. Wouldn't it be awful if he had to sell Mrs. Wiggins!"

"Well, the Beans are worried about it," said

Jinx. "Mr. Bean's going down to see Mr. Weezer, at the bank, to see if he can borrow some money. He said: 'Likely we won't have much besides beans to eat for a few years. But don't you worry, Mrs. B.,' he said; 'we've been through hard times before. We'll get by.'"

"It's worse than I thought it was," said Freddy. "We ought to go down right away and tell Mrs. Bean what we know."

"Wait a minute," said Mrs. Webb. "I know Mrs. Bean would listen to you, but wouldn't it be better if all the animals on the farm went down together? We're all concerned in it, and wouldn't that carry more weight?"

"I believe you're right," Freddy said. "I tell you what—we've got all afternoon to round everybody up and tell 'em about it; I guess we'd better call a meeting in the barn and tell 'em all at once. Then after supper, go over to the house. Come on, Jinx; we'll go down to the barn and run up the flag. You Webbs going down, too?"

"Yes," said Mrs. Webb, "I'd like to get the place tidied up a little before nightfall. That web was as neat as a pin when we left it last spring, but it beats all how much dust and dirt accumulates when you leave a place, even for a few days. I expect I'll have my hands full. But Webb can go to the meeting. He's only in the way, housecleaning time.''

So the Webbs climbed up on Freddy's nose, and they all started for the barn.

Chapter 5

Some years earlier the animals had formed the First Animal Republic, with Mrs. Wiggins as President, and Commander-in-Chief of its army, which under her leadership had fought two remarkably successful campaigns. In peaceful times there wasn't much governing or commanding to be done, but when any danger threatened, the old flag of the F.A.R. was hoisted on the barn. That was the emergency signal. When they saw it, or heard from neighbors that it was flying, it was the duty of all citizens to drop everything and hurry down to the barn.

As soon as Freddy and Jinx had warned Mrs. Wiggins and got the flag up, the animals began streaming in. There were field mice and woodchucks and chipmunks and rabbits from the meadows and pastures, and there were squirrels and porcupines and bears, and even a wildcat or two, from the woods. There was Sniffy Wilson, the skunk, and his family, and John, the fox, and hundreds of birds. And of course all the regular farm animals who lived around the barnyard. Even Old Whibley, the owl, had come down from the Big Woods.

The barn was crowded to the doors when Mrs. Wiggins called the meeting to order. "Fellow citizens," she said, "you have been called together to hear some rather disturbing news. Most of you are doubtless acquainted with that distinguished team of world travelers and explorers, Mr. and Mrs. Webb. They have just returned from Hollywood, and will no doubt later have much to tell us concerning the manners and customs, the follies, fancies and foibles of that—that glamorous—" Here Mrs. Wiggins, who had been slowing down gradually, came to a full stop. "Good land, Charles," she said, looking down at the rooster, "I can't remember all those big words. That was a real nice speech you wrote out for me, but I guess you'll just have to let me tell it in my own way."

Charles shrugged his shoulders crossly. "What a president!" he muttered to Henrietta. "No style; no sense of—"

"Shut up!" said Henrietta.

"Now the point is, folks," Mrs. Wiggins went on, "first, that the Webbs are back. Let's give them a big hand. Webb! Where are you, Webb? Come forward please."

Mr. Webb had already come forward and was perched on the tip of Mrs. Wiggins' left horn, but of course she couldn't see him, and she continued peering around anxiously for him all the time that the crowd was cheering and Mr. Webb was waving his legs at them in greeting. Mrs. Webb, too, had decided to let the housecleaning go, and had slid down to the other horn.

"Well," said Mrs. Wiggins finally, holding up a hoof for silence, "I'm sorry that the Webbs seem to have disappeared somewhere—"

"They're on your horns, cow," said a voice.

"Eh?" Mrs. Wiggins rolled her eyes to try to catch a glimpse of her horns. She rolled them up so far that she said "Ouch!" and shook her head. "I'll have to take your word for it," she said. "All I saw then was the inside of my head, and that's so dark that I couldn't see them if they were there."

"Dark and empty," Charles said sarcastically. And then he squawked, for Henrietta seized him by the ear and rushed him outside.

Then the cow went on and told them about what the Webbs had found out, and how the plan was for all the animals to go up to the house in a body and tell Mrs. Bean, and demand an explanation from Mr. Doty. But first, she said, they ought to talk it over to see that everyone agreed, or maybe had a better plan.

Usually when there was any general decision to be made there would be an endless amount of talk, and as many plans as there were animals present. But this was the most serious thing that had ever come up. They all knew the reason why Mr. Bean never had much money. Whenever he got a few dollars ahead, instead of saving it, he would put in some new improvement to make the animals more comfortable. Some people thought he spoiled his animals and his neighbors criticized him a lot, but you would have a hard time finding a farm where the animals were as contented as they were at the Beans'. And so when they heard the news they were good and mad, and they began muttering, and then shouts came from all over the barn: "Throw him out!" "Let's run him off the place!" "Down with Doty!" And then Charles flew up on the dashboard of the old phaeton. For he had sneaked back in again when Henrietta wasn't looking.

"Fellow citizens!" he crowed. "What are we waiting for? Are we to stand here idle while this false Doty, this serpent, this vile-hearted impostor, plots the fall of the house of Bean under our very beaks and noses? Even now he sits in the kitchen, grinning evilly and eating apple pie as he schemes our ruin. Well, we know what to do with traitors. Teeth and claws, comrades; teeth and claws! Forward, in the name of the F.A.R.! And *I* will lead you!" And he started for the door.

This was one of the shortest speeches Charles had ever made. Although he enjoyed nothing so much as calling on a large audience to rise and overthrow something or other, he seldom got around to demanding action—first, because he liked hearing his own voice, and second—well, there isn't any second. So when he actually started to lead the animals against Mr. Doty he took Freddy and Mrs. Wiggins by surprise. And the whole crowd had streamed out the door and headed for the house before they could prevent them.

"Great day in the morning, Freddy," said Mrs. Wiggins, "they'll spoil everything if they gang up on Doty before we explain to the Beans. We must stop them."

"How?" inquired a deep voice, and Freddy looked up. Old Whibley was sitting on a beam above them.

"I don't know," said the pig. "I guess we didn't handle it very well."

"You didn't handle it at all," said the owl. "Your scheme was no good in the first place. You can't prove that Doty isn't Mrs. Bean's brother, and that's the main point."

"But we've got to stop Charles," said Mrs. Wiggins.

"He'll stop himself, just like any alarm clock, whether it's got feathers on or not. My guess is he's run down already. Come out and see." And he dropped from the beam and floated out the door to perch on the clothesline.

The other two followed him. Halfway across the barnyard Charles had indeed brought his followers to a stop with an uplifted claw. "My friends," he was saying, "let us pause and con-

Forward, in the name of the F.A.R.

sider. In our righteous indignation we have perhaps been too hasty. My eloquent appeal has stirred your patriotism to its depths, and yet perhaps the hour for action has not struck. Understand me, I take nothing back of what I have said—"

"That's easy," Old Whibley remarked. "You haven't said anything yet."

Freddy ran around and faced the animals, pushing Charles to one side. "Look," he said; "Whibley thinks we haven't got much of a case against Doty yet. But just the same I think we ought to tell Mrs. Bean what the Webbs found out. Come up to the porch and sit down quietly. Charles, you keep your beak shut."

Charles' courage had revived, now that he saw that he wasn't going to have to lead any sort of attack, and he blustered a little. But nobody listened. Then when they were all sitting in a half circle around the back porch, Freddy went up and tapped on the door.

Mr. Bean opened it and looked out. "What in tarnation is going on here?" he demanded. "Mrs. B.," he called over his shoulder, "you sent out invitations for a party or something?"

Mrs. Bean came hurrying out, followed by Mr. Doty. "Land of love!" she exclaimed.

"Looks like a town meeting. What is it, Freddy?"

"It's a farm meeting, ma'am," said the pig. "We've found out something we think you ought to know, and we've come down to tell you about it."

So Mrs. Bean said to go ahead, and Freddy told her about the Webbs and about the meeting between Mr. Doty and Mr. Garble. While he was talking, Mr. Bean walked over to the corner of the porch and puffed so hard on his pipe that the sparks flew into his beard. He was very proud of his animals, but he never liked to hear them talk. He was sort of old fashioned that way.

Freddy watched Mr. Doty as his story went on. Mr. Doty didn't look at all disturbed; he looked amused, and every now and then he would nod his head and say: "Well, well, well!" as if in agreement. And when Freddy finished, he said to Mrs. Bean: "Well, well, Martha; quite a story, eh? 'Deed, 'tis so!"

"It's a very queer story, Aaron," said Mrs. Bean slowly. "I didn't know you knew Herb Garble."

"I didn't know him. Ye see," he said with a great appearance of honesty, "when the circus came to the town I was living in—Collywobble, Indiana, 'twas—and I saw that notice that somebody wanted Aaron Doty, I went in and asked Mr. Boomschmidt what it was all about. He told me. Well, I'm a poor man. If there was some money coming to me, I wanted it. That's natural, ain't it?"

"Of course it is," said Mrs. Bean. "But why did you never come before?"

"Well, well, I've been wanting to for years. Been wondering if you was alive. But—well, I guess I was ashamed to show up here all ragged and run down. And trips like that I couldn't afford. I couldn't even write, because you was always a real pretty girl, Martha, and I knew you'd surely married, and I wouldn't know your married name. And of course I didn't know that father had left any money."

Mr. Bean took the pipe out of his mouth. "Where's Garble come into it?" he said gruffly.

"Well, well, you don't like Garble, William. Nor neither do I. But if it hadn't been for Garble. . . . Well, I didn't have any money for the trip. And I was talkin' to a fellow I met in the circus—forget his name—one of the hired hands. Course, he knew Centerboro, with the circus coming here every year. He says: 'Write to Herb Garble. He's got lots of money. He'll grubstake you.' So I put in a long distance call right away to this Garble—"

"Where'd you get the money for a long distance call if you were broke?" Freddy asked.

Mr. Doty smiled, but Freddy saw the same mean look in his eyes that had been there when he had thrown stones at Uncle Wesley. "Generally speakin'," he said, "questions put by pigs I don't answer. Same as criticism by spiders I disregard. But I consider that my dear sister here will want an answer. So I'll just remark that I reversed the phone charge, and Mr. Garble paid at the other end. We struck a bargain, and he sent me my fare, and I came on."

"But why didn't you write to us, Aaron?" said Mrs. Bean. "We'd have sent the money."

"Well, well, so you would. So you would, I expect. But—oh, I was kind of ashamed of being so poor. I didn't want you to know about it. That's why I didn't tell you about Mr. Garble."

"He just thought up that one," Freddy whispered in Mrs. Wiggins' ear, and the cow nodded. But Mrs. Bean took hold of Mr. Doty's arm and squeezed it. "Why of course, Aaron," she said, smiling at him, "that was perfectly natural. Well, you don't have to worry about that any longer." She looked down at Freddy. "Your detective work has made you too suspicious, Freddy," she said. "Brother Aaron has given us a straightforward explanation, and I hope you see now that your suspicions were uncalled for. All you animals see that now, I hope?" she said, looking around at them.

The animals all nodded, though some of them still looked doubtful. Mr. Bean knocked out his pipe and came back to the front of the porch. "We'll all accept that explanation," he said. "But you animals! You're Bean animals. You live on this farm. You've got a right to ask questions. Remember that." Then he waved his hand to dismiss them.

"Three cheers for Mr. and Mrs. Bean," Freddy called, and the animals cheered.

"I think it would be nice if you gave three cheers for Brother Aaron, too," said Mrs. Bean. So they gave them, too, but they were pretty limp cheers.

When they were back in the barn, Freddy said: "I guess there is nothing more we can do right now. How many of you believe Mr. Doty's explanation?"

A number of the smaller animals put up

their paws, and Mrs. Wiggins' sister, Mrs. Wogus, raised a hoof. When some of those who had put up paws saw that, they put them down again, because everybody knew that Mrs. Wogus wasn't very bright, and was almost certain to be wrong.

"Oh, well," said Freddy, "you have a right to your own opinions. Personally I think Doty made the whole thing up. He's pretty good at making up excuses, you know. I don't think Garble is the kind of man who would pay for a long distance call from somebody he didn't know, or would send money to a stranger. I think he knew Doty before. But I can't prove it. Mr. Doty was too smart for us this time. But give me a few days, and maybe I can find out some things."

"Give Doty a few days, you mean," said Jinx angrily, "so he'll get the money and beat it. We ought to run him off the place!"

A good many of the animals agreed, but Freddy said: "That wouldn't do any good. You know how honest the Beans are. As long as Mrs. Bean thinks Mr. Doty is her brother, she'll give him the money, and whether he's in a deal with Garble makes no difference to her. Even if we proved him a crook, he's still her brother and so entitled to the money."

So Mrs. Wiggins declared the meeting adjourned, and the animals all went back home.

Chapter 6

Next afternoon Freddy started to walk down to Centerboro. It was a cool fall day, and as he trotted along briskly he began to compose a poem for the next issue of the Bean Home News. He was writing a series on The Features, and had already done the nose and ears, so he thought he would do one about the mouth. But each time, after two or three lines, Mr. Doty kept coming into it. The first one went:

The mouth is quite a useful feature;
With it, three times a day, you eat your

Meals, and with it, Doty produces
Big lies, and very lame excuses.

"Tut, tut," said Freddy; "I can't put that in the paper." So he started again.

The mouth, between the nose and chin,
Is used for (quietly) taking in
Both food and drink. Also for speaking,
For singing, hollering and shrieking.

But if you let it talk too much
You'll find it getting you in dutch,
For it, unless used just for grub, 'll
Cause you an awful lot of trouble.

And you will find, like Mr. Doty,
That—

"Oh, dear," said Freddy, "there he is again!" Then as a great clattering and roaring began in the distance and grew louder behind him, he looked around. "And there he *really* is!" he exclaimed, for Mr. Doty's car was coming down the road.

As Freddy stepped to the side of the road he saw that Mr. Doty was bent over the wheel, staring fixedly straight ahead. He came on, without looking to one side or the other, and perhaps he really didn't see the pig, for when the car was almost up to Freddy, it swerved and came straight at him. Freddy dove for the ditch and the car rattled by.

When he had scrambled back up on to the road he saw that the car had stopped and Mr. Doty was getting out. "Hey!" he yelled. "What do you think you're doing?"

Mr. Doty came up. "Well, well; apologize to you, Freddy. 'Deed I do! That old steering wheel! Take your eyes off it for a minute and it starts off somewhere all by itself." He shot a quick look at the pig. "Yes, sir," he went on quickly, "steering wheels, I just don't understand 'em. Chickens they go for, mostly. Never saw one go for a pig before. Well, well; hop in if you're going to town."

Freddy thought he would be safer in the car than out, and got in. There was so much noise, when they started, that conversation was impossible. When they got to Centerboro, Freddy directed Mr. Doty to the jail, for he was going to call on his friend the sheriff. Mr. Doty refused to drive in, but stopped outside the high iron gates. "Churches, yes," he said. "High schools, theatres, even sawmills—yes. But jails, no. Jails I can't enjoy."

"Have you been in jail?" Freddy asked.

Mr. Doty jumped slightly, then he said: "I've visited friends was staying in 'em. Poor fellows. Bolts on the windows and bars on the door. Or vice versa. Makes me sweat to think of 'em." And indeed big drops of perspiration stood out on his forehead.

"This jail is different," said Freddy. "The prisoners always hate to leave when their time is up." He pointed to the sign over the gate:

Centerboro Jail
"A Home From Home"

He waved to a group of the prisoners who were playing hopscotch on the lawn, and went in.

The sheriff was in his office, shining up his big silver star with an old toothbrush. Freddy told him about Mr. Doty, and then asked if there was any way of finding out if Mr. Garble had had a long distance phone call from Collywobble, Indiana, about two weeks ago. "Sure," said the sheriff, and he called up his niece, Nettie, who ran the telephone exchange. And Nettie said there never had been any such call.

Well, that proved that Mr. Doty had made up his whole story, but as the sheriff pointed out, it still didn't prove that he wasn't **Mrs.**

Bean's brother. "And that's the only thing that will stop them from giving him the money," he said. "I dunno what you can do, Freddy, but you got to work fast. Of course, maybe Bean can't raise the money; folks claim Doty's share is around five thousand dollars and that's pretty near as much as the whole farm is worth."

"Well, you know Mr. Bean," Freddy said. "If he thinks he owes it, he'll pay it, even if he has to sell the farm and go to the poorhouse."

The sheriff scratched his head. "Let me think," he said, so Freddy let him. But at last he said: "I ain't getting anywhere. Just giving myself a headache. I don't do much thinking nowadays, and I guess it's like any other game, you got to practice a lot to keep in trim. To be honest, Freddy," he said in a burst of frankness, "I don't believe I've had a new thought since 1912 when I decided to quit wearing a necktie. But if you have any thoughts, me and the boys will stand back of you. Just call on us."

Freddy decided he'd have to do any thinking that was done, so he started right in. He was thinking so hard that as he turned into Orchid Street he ran smack into a boy who was coming around fast in the other direction. Freddy was heavier than the boy, so the boy sat down hard.

Freddy helped him up. "Oh, it's you, Jason," he said. "I'm sorry; I was thinking."

"Well, you sure get quick results," said Jason. He was going over to the athletic field for football practice. "Everybody's so discouraged that I don't suppose there'll be many out. I hope there'll be enough of the scrubs to give us a workout. Come on along."

So Freddy went. He sat on the sidelines and watched the boys go through their signals, and then when seven or eight of the scrubs showed up, the coach, Mr. Finnerty, lined them up against the school team. But they weren't strong enough to be much good. The coach danced around and yelled at them, and went in and played different positions himself but even he, when the scrubs had the ball, couldn't gain a yard, and when the team had the ball it might as well, Freddy thought, be playing against a lot of field mice.

A cold wind had sprung up, and Freddy slipped into Jason's sweater which was lying beside him. There was a padded headgear on the grass, and pretty soon he put it on to see what it was like. And he had just adjusted it to fit him when Mr. Finnerty came over to him. "Hey, you—whatever your name is," he said.

Pretty soon he put it on to see what it was like.

"Get up and get in there. —Go on, no back talk!" he shouted, as Freddy tried to explain. "I didn't get you boys out here to sit and watch the grass grow." He grabbed Freddy by the shoulder and pulled him up. "Go in there with the scrubs, at left tackle." And he gave the pig a push.

"O K," said Freddy to himself. "Why not?" He knew quite a lot about the game from having watched it so often, and he ran out and crouched down in position just as Jason dropped back to kick. He watched the ball, and the second it was passed he plunged forward.

Now Freddy was not large, but he was compact, and weighed nearly twice as much as Henry James, the right tackle opposing him. And of course he was closer to the ground, particularly as he ran on four legs. Henry went right up in the air, and Freddy ploughed on, sideswiped another player and sent him sprawling, and hit Jason just as the ball touched his fingertips. Jason went down and the ball rolled off to one side where it was captured by one of the scrubs.

It was first down for the scrubs and they yelled their heads off. Freddy helped Jason up, and the boy grinned. "You been thinking again," he said. Then the coach came up and whacked Freddy on the back.

"You boys," he said, "that's the way I've been telling you to keep down when you hit the line. That was the prettiest blocked kick I ever saw." He swung Freddy around to face him. "You haven't been out before, have you? I'd remember you if you had." A startled look came over his face. "What—ah, what is your name?"

"Frederick Bean," said Freddy.

"Bean," said the coach. "M-hm." He backed away slowly. "Well—er, Frederick, I hope you'll come out regularly. If you keep doing as well, I'll put you on the team." He had stopped looking at Freddy; he rubbed his chin and shot quick glances at the pig from under his eyebrows. Then he suddenly shouted: "Well, come on! We'll let the scrub have the ball. They won it. Let's see what they can do with it."

Freddy was pretty sure that all the boys knew that he was a pig. Indeed, he knew most of them to speak to. But he was sure that they wouldn't say anything. Nobody raises objections to having a good player on his team. And for the same reason, Mr. Finnerty wouldn't say anything either. So he buckled down and played hard.

Of course he wasn't any good at catching or throwing passes, and anyway, he needed all his legs to run with. But his blocking and tackling were superb. The coach was delighted with him. "Golly, Freddy," said Jason, "if Mr. Finnerty will let you on the team, I bet we can work out some plays that will beat Tushville."

Freddy said he didn't think he could spare the time—he was working on an important detective case.

After a while Mr. Finnerty said that was enough for today, and he called the boys together to give them a little talk before dismissing them. It was then that Freddy noticed that Mr. Doty was watching the play. There was another man watching, too. He was a short, red-faced, pompous man, and now he walked towards them. "Oh-oh," said Jason in Freddy's ear, "here comes Mr. Gridley, our principal. He doesn't like football."

Mr. Gridley stopped some distance from the group. He never came close to anybody he was talking to, but always stood off several yards and shouted. "Mr. Finnerty," he roared, "have these boys done their home work?"

"I don't know, sir," said the coach. "That's hardly my problem, is it?"

"You know how I feel about this game," said Mr. Gridley. "A complete waste of time, and moreover there is no longer any interest in it except among a few. I have warned you before that unless their scholastic record shows marked improvement, I shall prohibit football in the Centerboro school."

"He knows perfectly well that we're all getting good marks," Jason whispered.

Mr. Finnerty started to say something, but the principal held up his hand. "Now, now," he roared, "no excuses! And another thing: one of you boys—you there!" he shouted, pointing at Freddy who was edging away. "Come here, sir! You were running on all fours! Disgraceful! I've always said that football is a game only fit for wild animals, but no boy in my school is going to behave quite so much like a wild animal as that."

"Well, well, well," said Mr. Doty, who had lounged up nearer, "I see you are not familiar with the game as it is played nowadays, sir."

"Who are you?" Mr. Gridley demanded.

"Aaron Doty, Ph.D. at your service, sir. Also an M.B.F., I am."

Mr. Gridley, who was not a Ph.D. himself, was impressed, and doubly impressed by the

M.B.F., which he had never heard of before. "You mean you approve of these ape-like antics?" he demanded.

"I not only approve, I applaud," said Mr. Doty. "Myself, I introduced these same antics at Yale, where I was captain of the football team for three years. Where for three years we won easily every game we played."

"You couldn't have won those you *didn't* play," remarked Mr. Gridley.

"We could have, but it was unnecessary," said Mr. Doty loftily. "So we never tried."

Mr. Gridley looked a little confused, and then he said angrily: "You could have won still more easily if you had gone into the game with clubs and pitchforks."

"Against the rules," Mr. Doty replied. "No weapons allowed. But there's no rule against running on all fours. They've even adopted it at Harvard this year."

Mr. Gridley was evidently at a loss for an argument, and while he was searching for one, his eye fell again on Freddy. A puzzled look came over his face. "You—boy!" he said, and adjusting his glasses, he peered at the pig. "You're not in my school!"

"Well—no, sir," said Freddy.

"Well then, what—" He stopped. "Great gracious!" he exclaimed. "You're not even a boy. You're a pig!"

Mr. Doty attempted to interpose again, asserting that the whole team at one famous college was composed entirely of pigs. But Mr. Gridley brushed him aside, ordering Freddy off the field.

There was nothing else to do. Freddy went, and Mr. Doty followed after a minute. "Want a ride home?" he said.

"Home?" said Freddy sarcastically, for it made him mad to have Mr. Doty refer to the Bean house as his home.

But Mr. Doty grinned. "Home is where the icebox is," he said. "Jump in."

They couldn't talk much on the way, but when they drove into the barnyard and the car had stopped, Mr. Doty said: "There's no rule against pigs playing, you know."

"There's one against people who don't go to school playing, though," Freddy said.

"There ain't any against pigs going to school," said Mr. Doty. "You ever been? School ain't so bad."

"I haven't got the time," Freddy said. "Say, what's M.B.F.?"

Mr. Doty grinned. "Member of the Bean Family. That's right, ain't it? A brother-in-law is a member, ain't he?"

"If he is a brother-in-law," said the pig.

"Meaning you don't think I am, hey? Well, well; try and prove it!" Mr. Doty got out of the car.

Thinking things over afterwards, Freddy was puzzled. Here was Mr. Doty, who was trying to get the Beans' money away from them, who had tried to run him down in his car. Undoubtedly a thoroughly bad character. And yet he was a lot of fun sometimes. "And he certainly tried to help me out with Mr. Gridley," Freddy thought. "Oh dear, I wish people were all one thing or all the other. There's that Mr. Gridley, too. All the boys respect him because he's just and honest. But none of them like him, because he blusters and roars at them. And I bet they all like Doty."

It was too much of a problem for Freddy. He went into his study and finished up his poem.

The mouth is located below
The nose, and is constructed so
That when it grins, it stretches wide
To touch the ears on either side.

This elasticity is handy
In eating pie, or hunks of candy.
Though hunks that stretch the mouth too tight
(By some considered impolite)
Require much earnest concentration,
And interfere with conversation.
In fact, there are extremely few
Who can, with charm, both talk and chew.
It's best to keep the two things separate;
When dinner's served, just salt and pepper it,
And for your conversation wait
Until there's nothing on your plate.

Chapter 7

That evening after supper Jinx came bounding up to the pig pen. "I've got some bad news, Freddy," he said. "Mr. Bean was telling old Doty that he'd have his money for him in a couple of days. Mr. Weezer, down at the Centerboro Bank, is going to lend it to him. We've got to stop it somehow. Mr. Bean will never be able to pay that much money back, and he'll lose the farm."

So they went right down to the cow barn to talk to Mrs. Wiggins. When she heard the news, she said: "Well, if this man is really Mrs. Bean's brother, it's awful hard on the Beans, but we've got no right to interfere. Because the money really belongs to him. I wish we knew."

"I don't see what we could do," said Jinx. "Unless we can prove he isn't her brother."

"We'd have a *right* to do something. I guess 'twouldn't be so hard to figure out what."

"I wonder if he's married," said Freddy suddenly.

"I've stuck around the house a lot since he's been here, and I haven't heard him mention it. Of course he wouldn't, would he?"

"Well, as long as he hasn't—" And Freddy outlined an idea that had just struck him. But Jinx sniffed, and Mrs. Wiggins only said thoughtfully: "H'm."

"Great enthusiasm!" said Freddy. "Look, all I want to do is find out if he's real or a fake. It won't prove anything, but if we know he's a fake, we can do something, as Mrs. Wiggins says. Well, I'm going to do it anyway."

Among the many disguises Freddy used in his detective work, the best was that of an old woman—probably because the bonnet hid his long nose, and the skirt came down to cover his trotters. With it he wore spectacles and black cotton gloves. So next morning he got these things together and carried them down to the Centerboro Hotel, and went in to see Mr. Ollie Groper, the proprietor.

Mr. Groper was a large fat man who never used a short word if a long one would do. "This here," he said as he shook hands, "is a most felicitous visitation. Proceed into my sanctum." He led the way into his private office, sat down heavily, and nodded towards a second chair. "The assumption of a semi-recumbent or quasi-horizontal position will sort of facilitate the interchange of observations."

Freddy said: "I need your help. I'd like to take a room in the name of Mrs. Aaron Doty. Here's her clothes, and I'm her."

"Investigating the transgressions of some malefactor, I presume?" inquired the hotel keeper.

So Freddy told him about Mr. Doty.

"Well," said Mr. Groper, "I guess you're cognizant of the fact that the entire resources of this here establishment—culinary, pecuniary, and—and dictionary, are at your service." He started to heave himself up out of his chair, then paused. "I'd sort of like to see you attired in these here habiliments of femininity," he said. So Freddy put them on.

Mr. Groper looked him over carefully. He began to smile and then to chuckle, and then to heave and rumble with laughter. The laughter seemed to be all inside him, and he shook until the chair gave several loud cracks. Then he got up.

"I have never," he said—and stopped. "In all my life," he said, and stopped again. Then he shook his head. "Words fail me," he said, and led the way, still shaking and sputtering, up to a vacant room. Freddy thought it was one of the finest compliments to his power of disguising himself that anyone had ever paid him, and perhaps it was.

Up in his room, Freddy telephoned the Bean farm.

When Mrs. Bean answered: "Good day to ye, ma'am," he said. "This is Mrs. Aaron Doty. Would ye be kind enough to be after callin' me dear husband to the instrument?" He spoke in a terrible Irish brogue, which would have made any real Irishman curl up in knots, but which seemed the best way to disguise his voice.

"One moment," said Mrs. Bean, and Freddy heard her say: "Aaron, there's a woman wants to speak to you. She says she's your wife."

There was silence for a minute, then Mr.

Doty's voice: "I'll not talk to her. See what she wants, Martha."

"But if she's your wife, Aaron!" Mrs. Bean protested. Then she said: "You never told us you were married."

"Well, well, reasons I had for that a plenty," Mr. Doty said. "She's a terrible woman; I want nothing to do with her."

Mrs. Bean hesitated a minute, then picked up the phone. "He says he doesn't want to talk to you," she said.

"Ah, himself is a cruel hard man, so he is," said Freddy sadly. "And him walkin' out and leavin' me five years ago come St. Patrick's Day without a penny in my purse nor yet the heel of a loaf in the cupboard, and not hide nor whisker of him have I seen from that day to this. But says I to meself: 'It's Centerboro he was born in, and he had a sister there, and the sister he'll go back to, for there's truth in the old sayin' that the bad penny always turns up, and a bad penny he is surely.' Five long years I was savin' up the money for the fare, and 'twas hard come by, what with scrubbin' other folks' floors and polishin' other folks' windys, but save it I did, and I'm here. And him sittin' there cozy and warm in the fine house ye have, ma'am,

Freddy telephoned the Bean Farm.

I'm sure, with his feet in the oven and a pot of strong black tea at his elbow, and not a word to throw to a dog, much less to meself that's his lawful wedded wife."

"Wait a minute," said Mrs. Bean, and she left the phone. This time Freddy couldn't hear what was said, but presently she came back. "I'm sorry," she said, "but he won't speak to you. Where are you?" And when Freddy told her, at the hotel, she said: "I don't understand this at all. If you're really Brother Aaron's wife—"

"And haven't I the fine engraved certificate to prove it?" said Freddy. "With both our names set to it, and a picture of two sweet little doves a sitting close together on a branch at the top, and well I remember how he used to say 'twas him and me. Och, I can hear him now! 'Well, well, well, Bridget,' he says, 'them doves we'll be, cooin' at each other all our lives long.' But sorra a coo I've had out of him these many years."

Freddy was going good, but Mrs. Bean cut him short. "Yes, yes," she said. "You stay there, ma'am. Mr. Bean and I will come down and see you this evening." And she hung up.

Well Freddy had proved his point all right.

If Mr. Doty was the real Mr. Doty, and not married he would have said so right out. If, on the other hand, he did have a wife, he would have talked to her, no matter how much he disliked her. But he had been afraid to come to the phone, although he had not denied that he had a wife. It was pretty plain that he was afraid of being confronted with the real Doty's wife, and denounced as an impostor.

Freddy had only put on the old woman disguise because he thought that Mr. Doty might come to see him. And that was exactly what Mr. Doty did. About an hour later Freddy heard the familiar roar and rattle of his car; it stopped with a loud bang; and presently there was a tap on the door and Mr. Doty came in.

Freddy had arranged himself carefully in a chair with his back to the window, his trotters in their black gloves folded in his lap, and his bonnet pulled well down. Against the glare of light he was sure that Mr. Doty could recognize him. Mr. Doty stood for a moment frowning down on him. "Well, well," he said, "so you're my wife?"

"Wife, is it?" said Freddy. "Be off with you, good man. A wife I am, but not to any wee wizened article like yourself."

"Well, you're nothing anybody would pin up, yourself, if it comes to that," said Mr. Doty. "But you claim to be Mrs. Aaron Doty, and I'm Aaron Doty, so—"

"So if you're Aaron," put in Freddy, "you've shrunk terrible. A fine big man my Aaron is, with the fine bushy whiskers on him, though a dirty scoundrel entirely. But I'm thinkin' you're likely a bit of a scoundrel yourself, mister, and so I'll be tellin' the Beans this evenin'."

"Telling them what?"

"That you're no more Aaron Doty than I'm the Queen of Sheba."

The mean look came into Mr. Doty's eyes for a minute, but then he sat down on the bed. "Well, well, that won't do you much good, will it?"

"It'll do this much good," said Freddy, "that Mrs. Bean'll put you out of the spare room and me in it. For it's the kind heart she has, the good woman, and she'll not rest in her bed nights thinkin' of her brother's wife, trampin' the wet and wintry roads—"

"How do you know so much about the Beans' spare room?" Mr. Doty demanded sharply.

"Och, she'd not be lettin' you sleep in the

stable, though that's where you belong, I'm thinkin'."

"Well, well," said Mr. Doty, "this is getting us nowhere. See here, ma'am, you came here to find your husband. He ain't here, and sooner or later you'll go back again, empty-handed. How's if I told you you could go back with a thousand dollars in your purse?"

"Make it two thousand," said Freddy.

Mr. Doty laughed. "Ha! So you're after Doty's money too! Well, I'm glad to see we can do business together. Now all you've got to do is sit tight here for a couple of days. I'll tell the Beans I've had a talk with you, and we've settled to go back west together when I get the money. They'll be wanting to see you—"

"I'll not see them," said Freddy. "It's best not. It's dreadful soft-hearted I am, and it's drownin' in me own tears I'd be at the sight of them, and I'd let the cat out of the bag entirely."

Mr. Doty agreed. "I'll tell 'em you're too upset at finding me to talk to anybody. I'll make some excuse. Then when I get the money I'll bring you your share and—we'll be gone."

They talked a little longer, but Mr. Doty

was very cagey. The money, he said, was some that Mr. Bean owed his brother-in-law; he'd heard about it and decided to impersonate the brother-in-law and get it. But as to who he really was, or his connection with Mr. Garble, he said not a word.

But Freddy was well satisfied. He didn't think for a minute that Mr. Doty had any intention of paying him the two thousand dollars. He'd probably have to pay Mr. Garble, because Garble must know who he really was. Freddy still didn't have enough proof to convince the Beans, but it was enough for the animals. They could fix Doty somehow.

After Mr. Doty left Freddy took off his disguise and walked over to the athletic field. When Mr. Finnerty saw him he came over to him. "I'm sorry, Freddy," he said; "I can't let you play. Mr. Gridley says nothing doing."

"I thought he would," Freddy said. "But suppose I was a regular pupil in the school? He couldn't say anything then."

"He wouldn't let you go to his school. And there's another thing: there's a meeting of the school board tonight at Mrs. Winfield Church's, and he's going to propose that they drop football entirely."

"Why, I know Mrs. Church!" said Freddy, brightening. "She's a great friend of Mrs. Wiggins'. Who else is on the board?"

"Why, there's Mr. Weezer, and Judge Willey—"

"I know them both."

"And that Herbert Garble—"

"Wow!" said Freddy. "I'm going to that meeting! I can maybe kill two birds with one stone."

"Which birds you going to kill?" Mr. Finnerty asked with a grin.

"Gridley and Garble," said Freddy. "I'll go see Mrs. Church now. Wish me luck."

"You're going to need a lot of it," said the coach.

Mrs. Church lived in the upper part of town in a big house which was built of red stone and had a lot of little turrets sticking up all over it with queer little rooms in them. Mrs. Church's husband had built it. He had been a rich banker, and he had built it that way because he was fond, like so many bankers, of playing hide and seek, and the dozens of little rooms were wonderful for that. He used to give big dinner parties twice a week, and after dinner everybody would play, and then there would be handsome prizes. Some people thought it was silly for a grown man to be playing such games, but they were usually people who weren't much good at it. After he died, Mrs. Church kept up the parties, which were now famous all over the state, and even the Governor, who enjoyed a good game of hide and seek himself, occasionally came down from Albany for them.

When Freddy rang the bell, Mrs. Church herself came to the door. "Why this is a delightful surprise!" she said. "And how are Mrs. Wiggins and her charming sisters? I haven't had time to drive out lately; I've been pretty busy since I got rid of all my servants."

Freddy followed her into the drawing room. "You got rid of them?" he asked.

"Sick of having them around. Really, Freddy, they're just a nuisance. I had six, you know, and I couldn't move without falling over one of them. They were everlastingly chasing me around and picking up after me, though there's nothing I hate so much as a too neat house. I tell you, Freddy, it takes too much time to have servants. You tell them what to do, and you could do it yourself in half the time. Same way with that cook I had. Cooks always serve a big dinner—think they must. And if you don't eat it they get mad. Maybe you want just crackers and milk but you have to eat a lot of stuff you don't want just to keep the cook happy."

"Cooks always expect you to eat at the same time, too" said Freddy. "That's what I wouldn't like. Sometimes I have supper at four, and sometimes as late as ten, depending when I'm hungry."

"That's right," said Mrs. Church. "Tonight I'm going to have peanut butter sandwiches and pickles and ice cream. Probably tomorrow night I wouldn't look at it, but that's what I want tonight. If you'll stay, I'll be very happy to have you. We'll have to eat early, because the school board meets here at seven-thirty."

"That's one thing I came to talk to you about," said Freddy. "I'd like to stay. Can't I help make the sandwiches?"

"I'll make them. You run down and get a quart of ice cream and charge it to me. No, better make it two quarts; it's no fun eating ice cream if it's all gone before you're so full you can't take another bite."

Chapter 8

Since no outsider can be present at the meeting of a School Board, Freddy stayed in the dining room when the board members arrived, and finished up what was left of the ice cream. He had told Mrs. Church over the supper table all about the football situation, and also of course about Mr. Doty. She was very much upset to hear that Mr. Bean was in danger of losing his farm. "I think, however," she said, "if we talk to Mr. Weezer after the meeting, maybe we can get him to refuse to lend Mr. Bean the money. At least we can get him to postpone lending it for a while. Bankers always listen to rich people, and as you know, I am pretty rich. If we can do that—well, maybe there are other things we can do later."

At half past eight Mrs. Church came for Freddy, and he followed her into the parlor where the board was meeting. Mr. Weezer and Judge Willey smiled and nodded, but Mr. Gridley frowned, and Mr. Garble started up angrily. "Really, Mrs. Church," he said, "I protest against turning this serious meeting into a barnyard frolic with pigs."

"Sit down, Herbert," Mrs. Church said calmly. "If I remember correctly, your last frolic with this pig very nearly sent you to jail. Now, gentlemen," she continued, as Mr. Garble sank back in his chair, "we have voted down the proposal of Mr. Gridley and Mr. Garble to do away with the football team. But the team, as you know, has a bad record. It has never won a game against Tushville, its chief opponent. My friend here, Freddy, has a proposition to make to you. If you accept it, I believe Centerboro will have a chance to win."

"Pah!" said Mr. Garble disgustedly.

Judge Willey looked at him. "Your contribution to the argument, sir," he said, "seems to me of remarkably little value. It gives me no reason to classify you intellectually above hoptoads, much less pigs." He turned to Freddy. "Let's hear your proposition."

So Freddy told them how he had happened to get into the football practice, and how the coach had said that with him they'd have a chance of beating Tushville. "Of course," he said, "I know I couldn't play unless I was a pupil in the school—"

"How does Tushville manage it?" Mr. Weezer asked. "You can't tell me some of those boys are in school. The left guard in that last game I saw had a full beard, and one halfback had his wife and three children cheering for him."

"I believe," Mr. Gridley said, "that they have an arrangement by which anyone can come into school one or two days a week for shop work, which, they say makes him eligible for the team."

"And there's nothing you can do about it?"

"I haven't tried to," said the principal. "There is little interest here in the game. And I disapprove of it anyway; it is a rough, unmannerly game—"

"So is life a rough unmannerly game," said

Judge Willey. "But about the only way you can get out of it is to go jump down a well. In my youth I played football. Do you consider me rough and unmannerly?"

"On the contrary," said Mr. Gridley with a smile. Freddy was surprised to see that he could smile.

"Well, Freddy?" said the judge.

"Why, all I wanted," Freddy said, "was to find out if I can't be a pupil in the school. And it's not just for football. I never had any edu‐cation. All I've learned I've taught myself—"

"And you've done a very good job," said Mrs. Church warmly.

"I consider you a thoroughly conservative banker," said Mr. Weezer.

"And a highly successful detective," put in the judge.

"And a confounded nuisance!" Mr. Garble grumbled.

Freddy grinned. "Thank you," he said, "and you too, Mr. Garble. If I'm a nuisance to you, I'm very much pleased."

"Well, Mr. Gridley," said Mrs. Church, "what do you say?"

"I'm sorry, ma'am," said Mr. Gridley. "Im‐possible."

"And why, may I ask?"

"Because he's a pig!" shouted the principal. "And a very clever pig, I understand. What do you think would happen to me at the next P.T.A. meeting, if I had to announce that a pig stood at the head of all his classes? Those parents would tear me to pieces."

"Not any smaller pieces than they'll tear you into if the team loses to Tushville again," said Mr. Weezer, "and they find out it's because you wouldn't take Freddy. Remember, all those parents were once pupils in this same school. They had a good team in those days. They're proud of its athletic record. They're ashamed now when they see it beaten sixty or seventy to nothing."

"But how could I admit a pig?" Mr. Gridley demanded.

"Legally," said Judge Willey, "I see no bar. Speaking as one familiar with our legislative system, I would be of the opinion that since there is not, I am quite certain, any specific prohibition against admitting pigs to schools, these animals, or other animals, assuming that they can pass the necessary examinations, have an inherent right to all the privileges which the schools offer to the young. Should, therefore, this pig elect to take the matter up in court, and protest your refusal, I should be compelled under our Constitution to rule that you must admit him, or face trial for contempt of education."

"Dear me," said Mrs. Church, "I'm afraid I —well, could you put that in words of one syllable for me, judge?"

"Certainly. Unless the law definitely says: No pigs, Freddy must be admitted."

Mr. Gridley shrugged his shoulders, and gave in. He turned to Freddy. "If you will present yourself at my office tomorrow morning I will give you the necessary examinations. If you pass them, you will be admitted to the school. And let me add that you need not fear unfair treatment; you will get the same examination, and the same treatment later, that I would give to any pupil in the school."

Freddy thanked him and everyone seemed pleased except Mr. Garble, who said "Pah!" again and jumped up and stalked angrily out of the house.

"Thank goodness he's gone," said Mrs. Church. "Now there is another matter which has nothing to do with the school, but which I should like to discuss."

"Then I'd better go," said Mr. Gridley, getting up.

"I think," said Mrs. Church, looking at Freddy, "that although it doesn't concern you, you might have some helpful ideas. Unless Freddy objects."

Freddy said he'd be glad to have the advice of anyone with such wide experience. So then Mrs. Church told them all Freddy had told her about the man who called himself Aaron Doty.

"Legally," said the judge, "I don't think you have a case against this man. Of course it is plain that he and Mr. Garble are trying to get the money by pretending that he is Mrs. Bean's brother. But your only evidence comes from the Webbs, and I do not think that a jury would convict a man on evidence given by spiders. Unfortunately, there is a widespread prejudice against spiders. Put a spider in the witness box, and what would your jury do? Would they listen to him? They would not. They would do just what they do at home—they would rise up and try to swat him with a rolled-up newspaper.

"Furthermore," continued the judge, "that evidence has been explained away by Mr. Doty. His evidence was not very satisfactory, but it was good enough for the Beans. I am afraid all you can do for the moment is prevent Mr. Bean from borrowing the money. That is up to Mr. Weezer and the First National Bank."

"And I am sorry to say," said Mr. Weezer, "that now that I have agreed to lend him the money, I can't back out. I respect Mr. Bean; I will do anything within reason to protect him from this impostor, and if I had known this before he came to me, I could have refused. But I can't now."

Mrs. Church looked at him and smiled. "In that case," she said, "I shall take all my money out of your bank and deposit it in our friend Freddy's bank, the First Animal. Furthermore, I shall explain this action around town by telling everyone that I no longer consider the First National a suitable place to keep money. I shan't say that it isn't safe, Mr. Weezer. Just— unsuitable. And as your largest depositor, I am afraid that it may have an effect on your other clients."

"It has on me immediately," said Mr. Gridley. "I shall tomorrow transfer not only my own money, but the school funds, to the First Animal."

"Oh dear, oh dear!" said Mr. Weezer distractedly. "That will never do! I appeal to you as a fellow banker," he said to Freddy. "You know what will happen if they do that."

Freddy said: "Yes, everybody will think that the First National isn't safe, and they will take all their money out, and you won't have any to lend to Mr. Bean."

"I won't have any bank!" Mr. Weezer moaned. He pulled out a large white silk banker's handkerchief, which had his initials intertwined with dollar signs embroidered in one corner. He wiped his forehead and said: "I shall have to tell Mr. Bean that I can't lend the money. I shall have to break my promise to him."

"You needn't refuse flatly," said Freddy. "Just put him off for a while—then maybe we can get rid of Doty some other way."

"I'll put him off a month," said the banker. "But if you can't get rid of Doty in that time, I'll have to let Mr. Bean have the money."

They left it at that. Freddy went back to the hotel for the night, then in the morning, leaving word that if Mr. Doty asked for Mrs. Doty he was to be told that she was out of town for a few days, he presented himself at Mr. Gridley's office. Except in arithmetic he did very well. "I still feel," Mr. Gridley said, "that this

Freddy was sure that none of the teachers would know the difference.

is very irregular, but I shall admit you to the school. You will report after lunch to Miss Calomel's room, and I shall expect you to be dressed like the other boys. You will receive fair treatment but I warn you that if you do not keep up your studies you will be dropped. Good morning."

Freddy thought he could keep up his studies all right but he had no intention of going to school every day. Fortunately his Cousin Weedly now lived on a farm close to town, and Freddy walked out to see him. Weedly didn't have to be persuaded. He thought it would be fun to go to school, and he agreed to take Freddy's place three days a week. Freddy had gone to the Busy Bee and bought two of everything just alike—pants, shirt, sweater and cap—and as pigs look a good deal alike anyway, except to other pigs, Freddy was sure that none of the teachers would know the difference, particularly as there was a close family resemblance between them; they both had the same pleasant, open expression.

So Freddy went to school that afternoon. Miss Calomel treated him just like the other pupils, and although the girls giggled a good deal at having a pig in the class, for which you can hardly blame them, everything went off well. Afterwards he went up to football practice. Everybody knew now that Freddy might play on the team, and half the school was there to watch. Mr. Finnerty was delighted.

"There hasn't been so much interest in football here in years," he said to the squad. "Indeed, there has been so little that I can't blame Mr. Gridley for wanting to stop it entirely. However, don't get the idea that we are going to pile up any big score against Tushville. Our team is still fifteen pounds lighter, man for man, than theirs, and though Freddy can rip up their line, and is better than anyone they've got at blocking, he can't pass and he can't catch; and what's worse, he can't run with the ball. Make no mistake, we've got a hard fight ahead of us."

"I've got an idea about that, coach," said Freddy. "I—" Then he stopped. Better say nothing in front of all these people, he thought. Don't want Tushville to hear about it. Spring it on them as a surprise, and if it works . . . !

"Tell you later," he said.

Chapter 9

Most people think of pigs as lazy animals. As a matter of fact they are probably right. But like most lazy persons, pigs work harder, when they do work, than more energetic people. They do this because they are anxious to get through the work as quickly as possible, so they can lie down and go to sleep again. At least that was the way Freddy figured it out. And for that reason, he said, they do just as much work in a week as energetic people and should not be criticized.

But Freddy didn't have much time to be lazy now. There was school two days a week; there was football practice nearly every afternoon;

there was the Bean Home News to get out every week, and the affairs of the First Animal Bank, of which he was president, to be attended to; and there was Mr. Doty. This last was of course the most important, and so he spent as much time as possible at home, conferring with his friends on plans to get rid of the impostor.

He had to go back and forth so much between Centerboro and the farm that he got out his old bicycle and oiled it up. His legs were too short to touch the pedals at the bottom of their swing, but he could push the bicycle up the hills and then coast down the other side, so that it was faster than walking. He lost a lot of weight in the first week or so and Mrs. Bean had to take in the waistband of his trousers three times.

He was pretty puzzled about Mr. Doty. Anyone who could cheat nice people like the Beans was certainly a crook, and a mean one. When he was not around, the animals talked bitterly about him and tried their best to think up ways to get rid of him. But when he was with them he was a lot of fun telling stories and thinking up games, and then they forgot that he was a crook and began to like him again. Mrs. Wiggins had said that they ought to pretend to like him, so that he wouldn't be suspicious of them. But they didn't have to pretend much. Even Freddy, when Mr. Doty came down to watch football practice, and made suggestions for improving the game, had a hard time remembering what a low-down sneak he was.

"I suppose," Freddy said, "that just as your friends have things about them that you don't like, your enemies have things that you do."

"The Beans are having the same trouble with him, only the other way round," said Jinx. "We've got to hate him, in spite of the nice things, and they're trying to like him, in spite of the things they don't like. I've heard them talking—they don't like his not getting up until ten o'clock. And he won't help Mr. Bean with the chores—says he's got a weak back, on account of he sprained it the day he won the international ski race. Huh! Only race he'd ever win would be when they ring the dinner bell."

"Say, that's an idea," said Freddy. "If you want to get race records broken, instead of firing a pistol at the starting line, you ought to ring a dinner bell at the finish."

Perhaps because the animals had this sort of sneaking liking for Mr. Doty, they couldn't seem to think of any way to get rid of him. And then of course neither driving him away nor proving to the Beans that he was a crook would do any good—he was still Mrs. Bean's brother. What they needed was proof that he wasn't Aaron Doty. The only clue they had was the lettering on the big trunk he had brought with him. C.B.—Freddy was sure these were his real initials, although on the first day he had explained them to the Beans, by saying that he had been with a Wild West show, under the name of Cactus Bill. And the trunk was kept locked, so that even the mice hadn't been able to look around in it.

But Freddy always worked on the theory that it is better to do *some*thing, than just to sit and wait. So he went into the closet where his disguises were kept, and picked out one.

Now Mr. Garble lived with his rich widowed sister, Mrs. Humphrey Underdunk, and one evening the two of them were sitting comfortably on the front porch, when a very small man in a bright checked suit much too big for him, came up the walk. It was so dark that about all they could see when he came up the steps and took off his hat, was that he had a heavy black beard and seemed to be completely bald.

Before he could speak, Mrs. Underdunk said

severely: "Go away, my man. We have nothing for you."

"Mebbe so," said the man in a hoarse and indistinct voice, "but I got somefing—pfff!—something for you. Pfff!" he said again.

Mr. Garble laughed. "Pfff! to you," he said. "What's the matter—swallow a mosquito?"

"Got an impef—an impediment in my speech," said the little man, and I guess we'd better call him Freddy, for you know as well as I do that that's who he was.

The truth was, he had two impediments. One was the pebble he had put in his cheek to disguise his voice, and the other was the beard, which wasn't fastened very tight over his ears, and kept slipping sideways and getting into his mouth.

"You're Garble, ain't you?" he asked. And without waiting for an answer: "My name's Doty—Aaron Doty."

"Doty!" Mr. Garble jumped. "Nonsense! I know Aaron Doty; he lives with his sister, Mrs. Bean, out west of town."

"So I've heard," said Freddy. "But he ain't Doty. Pfff! I'm Doty."

"Well, go be Doty somewhere else," said Mrs. Underdunk. "It's of no interest to us."

He seemed to be completely bald.

"Oh, let him tell his story," said Mr. Garble tolerantly, although Freddy thought his voice trembled a little. "So you're the real Doty, eh? Well, if all I hear is so, you'll get a nice sum of money if you can prove it."

"I can pfff—prove it all right, but my proofs ain't here, and it's no use going to the Beans, because I under-pfff—understand Mrs. Bean is satisfied that feller is her brother. That's why I come to fuff—to see you."

"Why me? I haven't anything to do with it."

"No, sir; but if I could put you in the way of making a thouff—a thouff—a thousand dollars—"

"Oh, good gracious, Herbert," said Mrs. Underdunk, getting up, "send the fellow away. Good heavens, man, you puff like a walrus."

"Yes, ma'am," said Freddy stolidly; "my mother was a walrus."

"Are you trying to be funny?" she said coldly.

"*I* ain't," said Freddy. "*You* was. My muv—mother's maiden name: Jenny Walrus."

"I've heard quite enough about you," said Mrs. Underdunk, and stalked into the house.

Mr. Garble laughed genially. "You mustn't mind my sister," he said. "She thought you were making fun of her."

"I was," Freddy said. "No walruses in my family. I just don't like folks laughing at my impeff—impeff—"

"Impediment," said Mr. Garble.

"Yeah," said Freddy. "Thanks. Well now look, mister. This feller calls himself Doty—I been inquirin' round town, and it seems like he's due for some money in a couple weeks. That money ain't his—it's—pfff!—it's mine. But I got to prove I'm Aaron, and I can't do it in that time, and then pffff! ffffft! off this guy goes."

"Pfff! Fffft! is the way he'll go all right," said Mr. Garble. "Excuse me. Well, where do I come into it?"

"Like this. My proofs—letters and such—are in a trunk in Mexico. I been livin' there. I sent for it, but it won't get here in time. So if you'd go to Mrs. Bean and tell her you know I'm the real Doty—"

"You'll give me a thousand when you get the money is that it?" Mr. Garble interrupted. "Well, for one thing I don't know it, and for another a thousand isn't enough. Make it two, and prove to me you're Doty, and maybe we can do business."

"O K for the money," Freddy said, "but if

I could prove it I'd be talking to the Beans instead of you. What you got to lose, mister? If I don't come through, you ain't out anything." And he thought: "Darned if I don't think I've got him! If he takes me up, he'll get rid of Mr. Doty, and then I'll just disappear and everything'll be all right."

Mr. Garble thought for a minute, then he said: "Well, I don't remember Aaron Doty, but I never heard that he was a dwarf. Come in the house and let's have a look at you."

"I'd rather not," said Freddy. "I got weak eyes—can't stand the light."

Mr. Garble got up and came close and peered into Freddy's face. "Say 'Pfff!' again," he said.

"What for?" Freddy asked, and at the "f" in "for" his beard blew right out straight.

"Ha!" Mr. Garble exclaimed. "I thought so!" And he seized Freddy by the collar and the seat of the pants and rushed him through the door into the lighted hall, swung him round, and snatched off the beard. "You!" he shouted. "By thunder, I've got you this time!"

Freddy, whose collar was still in Mr. Garble's grasp, tried to slip out of his coat, but the man shifted his grip and flung his arms around Freddy's shoulders. They wrestled for a min-

ute, each trying to trip the other. And just then
Mrs. Underdunk came out into the hall.

"For heaven's sake, Herbert," she said, "if
you want to waltz with this gentleman why
don't you—" Then she stopped. "Why, it's the
Bean pig!" she exclaimed.

"Go get the chauffeur," gasped Mr. Garble.

Freddy knew that when the chauffeur came
in, he would probably be tied up and put in a
crate and shipped off to Montana. Mr. Garble
had tried to do that to him once before. But his
suit hampered him, and he couldn't twist free.
So he suddenly went limp, slipped down
through Mr. Garble's arms, and lay motionless
on the floor. And then, before Mr. Garble had
the presence of mind to see through the trick
and grab him again, he jumped up and dove at
Mrs. Underdunk's knees, as if he were blocking
an opposing tackler on the Tushville team.
Mrs. Underdunk collapsed against the hatrack
with a shriek that was quickly cut off, as Mr.
Garble's overcoat was shaken from its peg and
fell down and enveloped her head.

Out of the corner of his eye, as he made for
the parlor door, Freddy saw the hatrack tip
slowly forward, and then come down with a
bang on top of her struggling figure. Mrs. Un-

derdunk was no friend of his, but as he galloped through the parlor he felt a little ashamed, and wished that he could stop and help her up. He had been well brought up, and he knew it was a breach of good manners to throw the furniture at your hostess, or even to knock her down. But his apology could wait. He ran through the front parlor and the back parlor and the dining room and the kitchen and out of the open kitchen door.

The cook was washing dishes in the sink. The sight of a dwarf in a checked suit, running on all fours through her kitchen, must have been rather unusual, but she merely glanced over her shoulder at him, then went on washing. But when he had gone she shook her head. "Guess I don't have to work in no circus," she said, and she dried her hands and went in and gave notice.

Outside in the shrubbery Freddy got his breath, and then plodded down to where he had left his bicycle, and rode home. "Darn that beard!" he said. "I almost had him. Well, I'll have to think of something else. I wish I hadn't swallowed that pebble."

Chapter 10

Since their return from the west, Mr. and Mrs. Webb had been giving a series of lectures on their experiences. Their voices were of course rather small for lecturing; they would only carry a distance of about two inches; but Freddy had twisted a big sheet of paper into a cone to make a sort of megaphone for them, and when they spoke into the small end, it magnified enough so that a dozen or so animals grouped about the large end could hear clearly. Mrs. Webb's lectures were *Hollywood From a Hat Brim,* and *Screen Celebrities I Have Met*

She was a talented mimic, and could entertain an audience for hours with her imitations of various movie stars. Her imitation of Betty Grable was extraordinarily lifelike.

Mr. Webb's talks were more serious: there was one on *How I Broke Into the Movies, With Practical Hints For Beginners.* Another, and a very thrilling one, dealt with perhaps their most dangerous experience, when they had been sucked up by a vacuum cleaner, whirled through into the dust bag, and had barely escaped with their lives. He also sang a few western songs in the manner of Gene Autry, and although he had neither a horse nor a guitar, everybody felt that he brought the very spirit of the open range to the platform.

The lectures were so successful that when Mr. Muszkiski, who ran the Centerboro movie theatre, read an account of them in the Bean Home News, he came out to the farm and engaged the Webbs at quite a large salary to come down once a week, on the evening when there was no show, to give them at his theatre. There was a microphone on the stage, and when it was turned up high their voices could be heard even in the last row of seats. Of course from the orchestra, their gestures couldn't be seen, and even the Webbs themselves were only tiny black specks, but at Mr. Muszkiski's suggestion, the audience all brought opera glasses and binoculars and telescopes, and when Mrs. Webb did her imitations, they stamped and cheered till the windows shook. Even the Beans came down one evening and made as much noise as anybody.

But of course the Beans were pretty unhappy, for the date was approaching when Mr. Weezer had to lend them the money for Mr. Doty. The animals noticed that Mrs. Bean no longer sang while she was doing the housework, and Mr. Bean no longer smoked his pipe, because he was saving money by not buying tobacco. It made them feel sad to see him without smoke puffing out of his mouth and seeping out of his whiskers; it was like looking at an abandoned factory chimney, and they began to turn against Mr. Doty. Fewer and fewer of them came to listen to his stories, and when he came out in the barnyard they turned their backs and walked away. When he noticed this, the mean streak in Mr. Doty came out. If a dog walked away without answering his whistle, he would call it names, and even throw stones at it. Perhaps he thought they were afraid of him.

But he was in a good deal more danger than he realized.

He did realize it a little when the animals began to play tricks on him. A dog would creep up behind him and bark suddenly, or if he held out his hand with a lump of sugar for Hank, the horse would put his head down and smell of it, and then bring his head up quickly to catch Mr. Doty a crack under the chin. Or a cow would switch her tail and whack him on the nose. Uncle Solomon, the screech owl, spent one whole night flying into Mr. Doty's window every half hour and giving his crazy laugh from the head of the bed. And always, wherever Mr. Doty went, even in his bed at night, there were ominous rustlings and whisperings and gigglings.

He complained to the Beans about it, and finally Mrs. Bean spoke to Freddy. "You animals ought to like me well enough to be nice to my brother," she said.

"We don't think he's your brother, ma'am," said Freddy.

"You must let me be the judge of that," she said severely. Then her face softened. "You know, Freddy, I have thought it all out. It could be that he isn't Aaron. But even if there was doubt in my mind—which there isn't—I'd have to give him his money. I couldn't run the risk of cheating my own brother out of his inheritance."

One afternoon—it was one of the days when Weedly had substituted for him in school—Freddy had just started football practice, when he saw Mr. Gridley beckoning to him from the sidelines. He ran over and said: "Yes, sir?"

"What are you doing here?" said Mr. Gridley accusingly.

"Why, I come out here every day after school," said Freddy.

"So I see," said the principal. "You come out even when you're supposed to be staying after school?"

Freddy guessed at once what had happened. For some reason or other Miss Calomel had told Weedly to stay after school. He was probably there now. "Golly!" he thought. "I'm in a spot! If he finds out that Weedly is taking my place—"

"You come back with me now," said Mr. Gridley.

There wasn't anything else to do. They walked back to the school together. At the door of Miss Calomel's room, Mr. Gridley started to go in, but the second his back was turned Freddy, instead of following, sneaked off quickly down the corridor. He went out and waited up the street that Weedly would have to pass through on the way home.

In about half an hour Weedly came along. "Hi, Freddy," he said; "say what's biting Mr. Gridley? I had to stay after school, and a little while ago he came tearing into the room, but when he saw me he said: 'How'd you get here?' Miss Calomel started to tell him I'd been there all the time, but he just turned around quick and stuck his head out the door and looked up and down the hall, and then he came back and said: 'Didn't you just come in here with me?'

"Miss Calomel said: 'How could he?' and I said: 'No, sir, I've been right here,' and then he looked kind of wild and dropped down into a seat and began mopping his forehead. Miss Calomel just stared as if she thought he'd gone crazy, but he didn't say anything; and pretty soon he got up and went back to his office."

Freddy told his cousin what had happened. "I guess Mr. Gridley must believe in ghosts," he said, "or he wouldn't have been so scared. If he does, maybe we'll get away with it. But

When he saw me he said, "How'd you get here?"

if he gets to thinking and finds out there are two of us—"

"Yeah," said Weedly. "Two Freddys would be pretty hard to take, specially if each one of 'em is only half educated."

"Well, if you have to stay after school again," said Freddy, "you must tell Jason so he can let me know. He's the only one I've told about us. I'll be going to school tomorrow; if Mr. Gridley doesn't say anything then, we'll be safe."

All pigs look about the same to people, although they look different to pigs. And evidently it never occurred to Mr. Gridley that there was more than one Freddy in school. He said nothing more about the occurrence, but he eyed Freddy almost fearfully when they met in the halls. Miss Calomel had her suspicions, because Freddy acted different on different days, and he seemed to have a terrible memory. Once she said: "Freddy, I think you're only about half here." Which was true; she was really only teaching half a pig. But she was a great football fan and wanted the team to win, so she kept her suspicions to herself.

The first game of the season was with Plutarch Mills, on October third, a week before Mr. Bean was to get the five thousand dollars

from the bank. The schools were evenly
matched; of two games the year before, Centerboro had won one, 6-o, and the other was a
tie. The team was driven over to Plutarch Mills
in the school bus, and half Centerboro piled
into cars and followed along, for everybody
knew by this time that Freddy was on the team,
and even those who weren't much interested
in sport were curious to see a pig play football.
The Bean animals, of course, attended in a
body, and Mr. Doty drove Mr. and Mrs. Bean
over in his car.

Mr. Finnerty had wanted to save Freddy for
the first Tushville game, the following week.
But he realized that if the Centerboro people
didn't see the pig play, they would be badly
disappointed. So he put Freddy in at once.

The Plutarch Mills boys had heard that a
pig was playing on the Centerboro team, and
while the players were warming up they
watched Freddy curiously. They decided that
he didn't look very dangerous, and they laughed
and kidded him a lot. Freddy didn't mind but
Jason got mad when Charlie Jackson, the
Plutarch captain, pointed to the C.H.S. on his
sweater and said: "What does that stand for—
Centerboro Hog School?"

"Sure," said Jason. "And P.M.H.S. stands for Pig Makes Huge Score. Ask me about it after the game."

As a matter of fact nobody piled up a huge score. Centerboro kicked off. The wind was against them and the kick was short. Charlie Jackson got the ball and started back, well protected behind strong interference, and the Plutarch Mills cheering section went wild, for Charlie was their fastest back.

Then Freddy drove in on them. Running on all fours, the pig was so heavy and so close to the ground that it was almost impossible to knock him over. Instead, one by one, the Plutarch blockers went head over heels. Then he made for Charlie. The boy tried to dodge, but Freddy was too quick for him. Of course he couldn't tackle, for his forelegs were too short to hold, so he just ploughed through Charlie and cut his legs from under him. The ball was jarred out of Charlie's grip and dribbled off to one side, where Henry James fell on it.

With the ball in Centerboro's hands on the Plutarch 40-yard line, Irving Hill, the quarterback, signalled for Jason to take the ball straight through the line, between left tackle and guard. He counted on Freddy to open a hole that Jason could go through. To the spectators, it looked as if the line had exploded. The opponents' right tackle and guard flew into the air, Jason followed Irving through the opening, and saw Freddy ahead of him, knocking off the backs, who were converging to tackle him. Jason made twenty yards before he was pulled down.

During the whole of the first quarter Irving kept calling for line drives, and each time Freddy broke through, and scampering about the field on all fours, bowled over the opposing tacklers, while Jason followed with the ball. When the quarter was over the score was Centerboro 23—Plutarch Mills 0, and the Bean animals and the Centerboro people who had come over to see the game had cheered so much that hardly one of them could talk above a whisper.

But Mr. Finnerty was not too well pleased. "You can't have Freddy play your whole game for you," he said. "For one thing, you'll wear him out before the game is half over, and for another, it's bad football to rely on just one man, or one type of play. You haven't punted, you haven't thrown a single pass, you've just plugged at that one spot in the line. I'm taking Freddy out. Now go in and use some of those plays you've been working on all fall."

After this the game was more interesting to watch. Plutarch Mills were becoming pretty demoralized, but with Freddy out they tightened up and pulled out two touchdowns in the second quarter. The final score was 30—14.

After the game the coaches and the captains got together. "We ought to protest your playing a pig against us," said the Plutarch coach. "But we've decided not to, and I'll tell you why. We're a weaker team than Tushville, and if we don't protest it will make them look pretty small if they do. So probably they won't. And what we want to see is that gang of Tushville bruisers get licked. We're all coming over to see that game."

"Well," said Mr. Finnerty, "you're good sports. But such a protest couldn't be made to stick anyway. Freddy's a regular pupil of the school. Tushville can protest until they swell up and bust, but it won't do them any good."

Chapter 11

The Plutarch Mills game caused a lot of talk, and sports writers all over the country commented on it. Some were pro-pig and some were anti-pig. Some said, what of it?—if a pig could be admitted to school, and could keep up with the children in his studies, why should he be debarred from free participation in athletics? Others said, what is the country coming to, when our school games are degenerating into brutal contests with wild animals, like the ancient Romans? But the national committee, which makes the football rules, decided to wait and see. "It will be high time to make a ruling," the chairman said in an interview in *The Times,* "when elephants and tigers are introduced into the game. Then of course we shall have to take steps."

During the next few days Freddy received letters from four colleges, asking if he planned to continue his education beyond high school, and hinting that scholarships might be available. But Freddy didn't pay much attention to them, for soon Mr. Bean would get his money from the bank. And the only plan he had been able to think up was such a desperate one that none of his friends thought that he ought to try it. But he did try it anyway.

He knew that Mr. Bean had already signed all the papers, promising to pay the money back, and that the money would be ready for him at the bank Friday morning. To keep Mr. Bean from getting to the bank early, Hank was to pretend to be too lame to make the trip to town; and to prevent Mr. Doty from driving his car in, the mice had gnawed holes in the two rear tires. So Freddy stayed at the Centerboro Hotel Thursday night, and very early Friday morning he went out and saw Weedly.

"Instead of going to school today," he told his cousin, "I want you to get down to the Busy Bee, in your school clothes. Be there as soon as the store opens, and go in and walk around

"I want you to get down to the Busy Bee in your school clothes."

where everybody can see you. I want a number of people to think that I am in the store all this morning. Stay till about eleven, then beat it home and hide your clothes. Got that?"

When Weedly had agreed, Freddy went back to the hotel and telephoned Mr. Weezer's house. When the banker came to the phone, Freddy made his voice very gruff. "This is Bean," he said. "Got that five thousand ready?"

There was a pause, and a faint rattle, which Freddy knew was Mr. Weezer's glasses falling off, as they always did when any sum of money larger than ten dollars was mentioned. Then Mr. Weezer said: "It will be ready for you as soon as the bank opens."

"Well," said Freddy, "this tarnation horse has gone lame, and Brother Aaron's car has blown up, so I can't get down. I'm sending my pig, Freddy for it. You give it to him?"

"Dear me," said Mr. Weezer, "it's rather irregular. However, as Freddy is a banker himself, I won't make any difficulty about it."

So when Mr. Weezer opened the bank, Freddy was waiting. He got the five thousand and walked out of the bank with it pinned into his inside coat pocket. And after that nobody saw him for quite a while.

But as soon as Freddy left the bank, Mr. Weezer got worried. "I had a feeling," he said afterwards; "I just had a feeling that something was wrong." He thought of Freddy walking up the road, carrying all that money, and he thought of robbers hitting Freddy on the head, and of cars which ran over Freddy, and bolts of lightning which struck him—and he got in his car and drove out towards the Bean farm. He was surprised that he didn't overtake the pig on the way, and he was more surprised when Mr. Bean told him that he hadn't sent Freddy for the money, and he was just plain flabbergasted when after an hour's wait Freddy hadn't shown up.

Well, there was a lot of excitement, and during the day it spread out from the farm in all directions, until everybody in the county was talking about the pig that had robbed a bank. The Beans questioned all the animals, but most of them didn't know anything anyway, and those that did kept quiet. They phoned all Freddy's friends in Centerboro, but nobody had seen him. They called the state troopers, and the sheriff, who got together a posse to hunt for Freddy. But not a trace of him could they find.

The Beans felt pretty bad. Mrs. Bean sat at the kitchen table and cried and wiped her eyes on her apron, and Mr. Bean stamped up and down, chewing on the stem of a cold pipe. "That consarned pig!" he muttered. "Just like one of the family, he was. I'd 'a' trusted him with my last cent!"

"Well, he's got our last cent," said Mrs. Bean, "but I can't help thinking that maybe we ought to go on trusting him. Maybe he had some good reason for taking the money."

"Fiddlesticks, Mrs. B!—if you'll excuse my saying so," Mr. Bean growled, and Mrs. Bean began to cry again.

"Well, well, Martha, don't take on so," said Mr. Doty soothingly. "Told you time and again, that I ain't in any hurry for my money."

"Good thing you ain't," said Mr. Bean. "Where we'll get any more now to pay you with is beyond me. That consarned critter!"

Mr. Doty shook his head. "Pigs I never took to," he said. "Dogs and horses, yes. Even elephants, yes. But pigs, no. And this Freddy. Tried to stir up trouble for me the minute I got here. Oh, he's smart all right—smart as a whip, and just as likely to snap back and hit you in the eye. Did I ever tell you about the pig ranch I had in Wyoming? It was—"

"No," snapped Mr. Bean. "And don't be-gin."

Down in the village the story of the robbery was in everybody's mouth. And as it was re-peated, it grew. Freddy had held up the bank cashier at the point of a pistol; he had shot Mr. Weezer, grabbed the money, and run out and driven off at high speed in a large black limou-sine. Four pigs, armed to the teeth, had entered the bank, tied everybody up, blown open the vault with dynamite, and got away with hun-dreds of thousands of dollars.

Most of Freddy's friends in the village re-fused to believe these stories. They went around saying "Nonsense!" in a loud voice whenever they heard a new one. But it didn't have much effect. Mrs. Winfield Church, however, who had pretty well guessed what Freddy was up to, didn't say anything. That evening she went down to the jail.

The sheriff opened the door. "Why, good evening, ma'am," he said, and then he blushed. "You'll excuse my appearance," he said. "Just step into the drawing room and I'll go put on a necktie."

"You'll do nothing of the kind," she said, "I

don't want your party manners, I want you to tell me the truth. You're a friend of Freddy's, aren't you?"

"Sure am," said the sheriff. He followed her into the drawing room, and then stopped short. "Guess we'd better sit in the office," he said. "The prisoners were playin' football in here yesterday when it was rainin'. Taken a great interest in the game since the school beat Plutarch Mills. I ain't had a chance yet to pick up after them, with this posse and all."

"I don't like an orderly house myself," said Mrs. Church. "Doesn't look lived in." She picked up a chair that was lying on its side and sat down in it.

The sheriff pushed aside a broken lamp and set up another chair opposite her. "Well, ma'am," he said, "you're askin' me about Freddy. You know it's my duty to arrest him if I can find him."

"Yes. You needn't be afraid I'm going to tell you where he is. Anyway, I don't know. Not that I don't think he'd be safer in the jail than out hiding somewhere. You've got Herbert Garble on your posse, haven't you?"

The sheriff said he had to have him, he was one of the regular deputies.

"I see. But you know what he'd do if he found Freddy, don't you?"

"Well, I issued Herb a gun, and I kind of imagine he'd point that gun at Freddy and pull the trigger."

"Well, good heavens, man," Mrs. Church began; then she saw that he was smiling. "Oh," she said, "I see. You mean the gun wouldn't go off."

"Oh, yes it would, ma'am. It would make a real nice loud bang. But it wouldn't make any holes in our young friend, because I took care to load it with blanks before I gave it to Herb."

Mrs. Church laughed. "That relieves my mind a good deal. But now, what are we going to do about Freddy? He'll be caught and Mr. Doty will get the money and the only thing Freddy will have accomplished is to get himself sentenced to jail for a year or so for robbery."

"Ma'am," said the sheriff, "I'd be proud and happy to have Freddy in my jail. These prisoners are a nice lot of boys, but they didn't any of 'em get beyond the third grade. I don't say they ain't bright, some of 'em, but they ain't got much conversation. And I do like good conversation. Now with Freddy here—" He broke off as some giggling that had been going on outside in the hall got louder. "Come in, boys," he called. "Don't stand outside there snickerin'."

Three or four of the prisoners came in and were introduced to Mrs. Church. "I'm very glad to meet you," she said. "Are any of you burglars? I've always wanted to meet a burglar."

The others pushed Red Mike forward, and he said bashfully: "I used to do a little in that line."

"Did you enjoy it?" Mrs. Church asked.

"Well, yes and no, ma'am. It's a nice job some ways. You meet lots of people, but they're mostly asleep. Or else chasing you. I give it up finally and got a mail box."

"A mail box?"

"Yes, ma'am. I stole one, and I used to tie it on a lamp post on Main Street, and then leave it there a few days until it got full of letters. Then I'd empty it and peel the stamps off the letters. Trouble was, I had to deliver the letters myself then. It didn't hardly pay me for my time."

"I should think not. Well," she said getting up, "I must go along."

"Excuse me, ma'am," said a tall thin prisoner, "we—that is, Dirty Joe has just made a chocolate layer cake, and we was wondering if maybe you wouldn't like to have some with us before you go.''

''I can think of nothing I'd like better,'' she said heartily, and sat down again. So they got plates and forks, and straightened up the room, and then they all sat down and had the cake. And while they ate they talked about Freddy. All the prisoners liked him, and were sorry he was in trouble. And when Mrs. Church finally left, they assured her that if there was anything they could do to help him, she had only to let them know.

''I don't know when I've had such a pleasant evening,'' she said to the sheriff. ''You must all come to my house some evening and have a game of hide and seek. Burglars ought to be specially good at that.''

''We'll look forward to it, ma'am,'' said the sheriff.

Chapter 12

On Saturday the hunt for Freddy continued. The state troopers, who didn't know Freddy, and to whom all pigs looked pretty much alike, arrested every one they saw. They arrested thirty-four pigs on Saturday. There was a constant stream of police cars driving up to the Bean house with handcuffed pigs sitting beside the drivers. Then Mr. Bean would look at them and say they weren't Freddy, and they would be let go. Some of them were arrested two and three times, and they were pretty sore about it. The troopers were sore too because they got kidded a lot; people would watch them drive by and call out: "Oh, look at the two pigs!" or "Which one is the trooper?" and such things. They would have quit, if Mr. Bean hadn't offered a reward. He had signs printed and stuck up all over the countryside.

$5.00 Reward
For information leading
to the Arrest of this Pig

Bank Robber
When last seen was wearing
brown pants, green cap, blue
sweater. Height, standing on
hind legs, about 4'4". May
be armed!!
William F. Bean

Of course everybody that saw a pig called up Mr. Bean right off. He kept Hank harnessed to the buggy all day long, and as soon as a call came in he drove out to look at the pigs. He drove miles and saw more pigs than you would think possible, but he didn't see Freddy. He saw so many that he dreamed of pigs all night long.

Freddy, as a matter of fact, after leaving Centerboro with the money, had circled around by back roads and holed up in the old Grimby place in the Big Woods. This was the deserted house where the animals had once fought and conquered the terrible Ignormus. It was all falling to pieces, and no one ever went there any more—indeed, most people had forgotten that there was such a house. But the animals all knew it. It was a good hideout, because it was near the farm, and Freddy had posted sentinels to warn him if anyone approached. J. J. Pomeroy watched by day, and Uncle Solomon by night.

Saturday night, Jinx came up to give Freddy the news. "Boy, is Mr. Bean sore!" he said. "It's the sausage factory for you, kid, if they catch you. I brought you one of the signs he stuck up."

Freddy lit a match and looked at it. " 'Tisn't very flattering," he said.

"We all like it," said Jinx. "I don't know

where they got it, but everybody says it looks more like you than you do yourself. Of course it depends on what flatters you. If you'd rather have it look *less* like you . . ."

"Oh, shut up," said Freddy. "Why couldn't they have used the one that Mr. Wiese drew for Mr. Bean that time he came out? I just would like to have the picture do me justice."

"Justice, hey?" said the cat. "You sure would kick if it did that!" He grinned, and then said: "But say, what did you do with the money?"

"Tied it up, and J.J. hung it up in the top of that yellow birch at the corner of the Grimby house. I guess you ought to tell Mrs. Wiggins and Hank, but I wouldn't tell too many of them. They won't give me away, but someone might let it slip. Like Charles—he's an awful loose talker when he gets going."

Before he left, Jinx told Freddy about that afternoon's football game. The South Pharisee team had won, 6—o. "The boys sure missed you," he said.

"My goodness," Freddy said, "I forgot all about it. Well, I guess my football days are over. Mr. Bean can't raise any more money so I'll have to stay here till Doty gets sick of waiting for it and goes away. But even after I give it back, Mr. Bean will still be mad at me. He won't want me around." He sighed heavily. "I shall be just a wanderer on the face of the earth."

"You won't wander far if the sheriff's after you," said the cat. "He may be a friend of yours, but he sure works that posse hard. Well, so long, pig. Be sure and lock the front door."

Of course there wasn't any lock, there wasn't even any door; but Freddy felt safe with Uncle Solomon on guard. He slept that night on a pile of old sacks in the Grimby attic.

When he went out next morning, he found that Mr. Pomeroy, who was to relieve Uncle Solomon on guard duty at sunrise, hadn't shown up. What had happened, he found later, was that the robin had mislaid his spectacles, and rather than take the time to hunt for them, had started without them. As a result he had flown into a tree and sprained a wing. Unable to fly, he had set out to hop home, where he could get Mrs. Pomeroy to fly up and take his place. But by the time Mrs. Pomeroy got there the excitement was all over.

So Uncle Solomon had to stay on duty, and he was pretty cross about it. But as his crossness took the form of a grumpy silence, Freddy didn't mind, for the screech owl was sometimes a trying companion. He loved to argue and there was hardly anything you could say that he couldn't find an argument against. And then if you finally got worn out and agreed with him, he would turn right around and take your side and argue against you again. He was the only person Freddy knew who could win both sides of an argument.

Freddy had been thinking a good deal about what was going to happen to him. He didn't think Mr. Bean would ever let him come back to the farm. He would indeed be a wanderer on the face of the earth. But the more he thought about it, the more the idea pleased him in a mournful sort of way. It made him, he felt, a very romantic figure, leading a sad, gipsy life, a lonely pig, with a secret sorrow in his heart.

As it was Sunday, Freddy didn't think the sheriff's posse would be out looking for him. He thought he would walk down to the pool where Theodore lived. For he had it in mind to write a poem about the gipsy pig, and some of his best poems had been written on the grassy bank beside that pool.

So he went down through the Big Woods, followed by the watchful but grumpy—and by now, rather sleepy—Uncle Solomon. He crossed the back road, and walked along through the green silence of the Bean woods, murmuring the words to himself and beating out the rhythm with one fore-trotter.

Theodore was glad to see Freddy. "They haven't c-captured you yet, I see," he said. "Well, you don't have to bub-bub, I mean bother about the troopers. They've given up, according to what I hear. Too busy answering mail. I understand they had eight mail sacks full of letters last night, from people all over the country who think they've seen you and want the reward. There was even a b-batch of air mail letters from California. They claim it would take eight years to investigate all these pigs."

"That's the trouble with detective work," said Freddy. "Too many clues are worse than none at all." He sat down beside the pool. He wanted to recite his poem to Theodore. But you can't just say: "Want to hear my new poem?", because maybe the other person says No, and then you recite anyway and he gets mad. So he said: "Learned any new songs lately?" For Theodore had quite a fine bass voice, and he collected songs, the way some people collect stamps. He had some very rare old songs that went way back to the sixteenth century—and the nice thing about them was, he said, that they didn't cost anything, and that you always had them with you, and didn't have to protect them against burglars, because nobody could burgle your head.

If the frog had said Yes, Freddy would have had to listen to the new song. But he said No. So Freddy said: "Well, I was just thinking—there's a little thing of mine—oh, it's nothing much—but I was thinking if it was set to music—" And he began hastily to recite.

"Through the night, through the dark, through
   the rain and sleet,
   By hill and valley and plain,
Plods the wanderer pig, on weary feet—"

"And his poetry gives me a pain," interrupted Uncle Solomon, from his lookout on a branch above the pool.

"Oh, keep still!" said Freddy.

   "And his tears they drip like rain,"

he concluded.

"Personally," said Uncle Solomon, "I prefer my version. It avoids the use of the word 'they,' which is unnecessary, and it is more solidly constructed. However, as you were no doubt about to point out, it is a criticism of your poem, which, just as it is, heaven knows, is at the moment out of place. H'm, let me see. How's this? 'The pig with the infantile brain.' More descriptive. I assume, of course, that it is yourself whom you are describing and not some other pig, to whom it might not apply."

Theodore giggled, but Freddy shrugged and went on.

"And he sighs, and he moans, and his head
bends low,
And his tail has come uncurled,
For he has neither mansion nor bungalow—
Not a home in the whole wide world.

"Got you that time!" he said with a triumphant glance at the owl, who evidently hadn't been able to think of a rhyme quick enough.

"Not a home, not a friend, no uncles or aunts,
No brothers or sisters or cousins—"

"Not a coat, not a vest, not a pair of pants,"

said Uncle Solomon.

"O K, you're so smart; finish it," said Freddy.

. . . and he began hastily to recite:

"I merely suggest," said the owl; "I do not complete. I know quite well that there is only one correct rhyme to 'cousins'. It is 'dozens.' "

Freddy expressed surprise. "I didn't know you knew so much about poetry."

"I know a great deal about words. It is not the same thing. However, proceed."

Freddy went on.

"Though happier pigs, as they sing and dance,
Have relatives by dozens."

"Personally," said the owl, "I have not found that a multiplicity of relatives is conducive to gaiety. But continue."

"For others, the lights in the windows gleam,
For others, the fried eggs sputter;
For—"

"For the pig, all puffed up with self-esteem,
A roll in the muddy gutter."

And Uncle Solomon gave his dry little titter. "Rather neat, I think. Your mention of food suggested the roll though in general I consider puns rather vulgar."

"What was your verse, Freddy?" the frog asked.

"For others, the coffee with lots of cream,
And the toast, with lots of butter."

"It has always struck me as significant," remarked Uncle Solomon, "that in all poetry written by lower animals—I distinguish them thus from humans and from birds—there is an intense preoccupation with food. For your benefit, Theodore," he said, looking down at the frog who had his mouth open, and was scratching his head with his little green fingers, "I will elucidate."

"You needn't bub-bother," said Theodore.

"It is no trouble," said the owl graciously. "I suggest merely that the chief interest of the lower animal is food. His mind seldom rises to higher things. His eyes, if I may so express it, are on the dinner table, rather than lifted to the stars. The poem to which we have just been privileged to listen illustrates this very clearly. This pig, this friendless outcast—why do his tears drip like rain? (And I may remark parenthetically that tears dripping like rain is a very ordinary and hackneyed expression.) "

"Maybe you could improve on it," said Freddy crossly. He sometimes rather enjoyed these arguments with Uncle Solomon, but nobody likes to have a poem he has just made pulled to pieces.

"I could," said the owl. "If you say: 'By hill and valley and mountain, His tears they flow like a fountain.' Or: 'By hill and valley and highland, His tears turn him into an island.' But to return to my theme. The pig weeps. Does he weep for his friends, for his vanished home? Mildly—yes he does—mildly. And with —I may remark—a quite sickening sentimentality. But it is the food that really gets him going. He weeps for food—rich food. And that, I submit, quite proves my case. I will say nothing of the dreadful false modesty of our poet, who—"

He stopped short. They had all been so occupied with his remarks that they had not heard the rustlings and snapping of twigs in the woods behind them. But at that moment, Mr. Garble stepped out from behind a tree. "I've got you this time, pig," he said, and pointed a large pistol at Freddy's head.

Chapter 13

When Mr. Garble had learned from Mr. Doty that Freddy suspected them of plotting to get Mr. Bean's money, he was pretty nervous. And when Freddy called, pretending to be the real Aaron Doty, he had got good and scared. He had a lot of respect for Freddy's detective ability, and he saw trouble ahead. When Freddy took the five thousand dollars and disappeared he saw his chance. He joined the sheriff's posse.

The sheriff knew pretty well what Freddy was up to, but it was his duty to catch him if he could. He and his men had combed the country around the Bean farm pretty thoroughly, but they had not yet gone into the Big Woods. Mr. Garble wanted to search them on Sunday, but the sheriff had said No, Sunday was a day of rest. "I don't ever chase criminals on Sunday," he said. "As a matter of fact, I don't see why a criminal shouldn't get Sunday off as much as anybody else."

So Mr. Garble went out alone. He came down from the north through the Big Woods, and searched the Grimby house, and having found no clues, kept on and cut across the back road just about where Freddy had. It was then, as he was working down through the Bean woods, that he heard voices. He crept forward, and there at the pool he saw Freddy.

Of course Freddy didn't know, when Mr. Garble's pistol was pointed at his head, that it wasn't loaded. So he just stood very still. There was a plop as Theodore dove into the pool. But the owl didn't stir.

"O K." Mr. Garble motioned up the hill with his pistol. "After you, my fat friend."

"But-but why are we going this way?" Freddy asked. For he supposed that Mr. Garble would take him down to the farmhouse, then call the sheriff.

Mr. Garble showed his teeth in a sneering smile. "Why it's such a fine day, that I thought we'd go for a little ride. And then, instead of being locked up in a stuffy jail, I've planned a trip for you. A nice long trip. You're going to see the Great West—won't that be nice? —Now get going!" he snapped.

So Freddy turned and went. He felt pretty sick. He wasn't going to be any wanderer on the face of the earth. He was going to be nailed up in a crate and shipped off to Montana. This time Mr. Garble was going to succeed. For he didn't see any escape. His verses seemed pretty silly now; instead of weeping, a wanderer pig ought to be kicking up his heels and singing for joy. But it shows how low he was that he didn't give a thought to changing the poem.

In the meantime, Uncle Solomon after waiting to see in which direction Freddy went, had dived into the air and was winging it straight as an arrow for the cow barn. He was there in a matter of seconds. "Freddy is captured!" he called as he shot in the door. "Garble's taking him up through the Big Woods toward Schermerhorns'. Up and after 'em! Come on—everybody out!"

There was no time to raise the flag and call the animals together. As the cows trotted out of the barn and started up the lane, the owl flew off to warn the dogs and Hank and Bill and whoever else was in the barnyard. But he didn't think the rescue party could do much. Garble probably had his car somewhere near the Big Woods; he would have Freddy in it before they could catch him; and anyway, he had a pistol. There was one thing that might help, though. As soon as he had given the alarm, he started for Centerboro.

On the way he reproached himself bitterly, for he was really very fond of Freddy. "Solomon," he said to himself, "you have been inexcusably lax and remiss and negligent. It was your duty to keep watch for the enemy; instead, you abandoned that duty for an argument about an inferior poem. You are a fool, Solomon; a corrupt and perfidious traitor, a rogue, a scalawag, and a black-hearted, pie-eyed dope." It shows how upset he was that he used several slang words in his denunciation of himself.

When the owl flew in the office window, the sheriff was leaning back in his big chair with a toothpick in his mouth and his eyes closed.

"Sheriff!" Uncle Solomon called in his quick gabble. "Garble's got Freddy! Come on—hurry up or we'll be too late!"

The sheriff slowly took the toothpick from his mouth and said sleepily, and without opening his eyes: "Too late? You mean for church? Well now, that's too bad. Guess we can't go. Don't want to disturb everybody, comin' in late." And he went to sleep again.

Uncle Solomon flew over and perched on his shoulder and gave a loud screech in his ear.

The sheriff started up. "Hey now, look," he said, "that ain't any way to act. I told you at breakfast, Looey, I didn't think I'd ought to go today. On account of my Adam's apple durin' the singin'. I—" Then at last he caught sight of the owl. "Hunh!" he said in a puzzled tone. "You ain't Looey."

"No, and I'm not urging you to go to church," said Uncle Solomon. "I am requesting in words of one syllable to *hop to it!* Garble's captured Freddy."

At that the sheriff finally woke up all over. And two minutes later, with the owl beside him on the front seat, he drove out of the jail gate.

The sheriff shouted above the noise of the engine. "If Garble's kidnapin' Freddy, I know where he'll head for—his shack at the east end of the lake. His road crosses this one a couple miles up. If we're in time we'll cut him off at the corners."

When they reached the corners there was no sign of Mr. Garble. Uncle Solomon circled up in a spiral, hovered for a moment then shot down again. "Something going on up this left-hand road. Can't make out just what, but—" The rest of the sentence was lost in the roar of the engine as the sheriff swung the wheel to the left and shoved down the accelerator.

While all this was going on Theodore had not been idle. As soon as Freddy and Mr. Garble left the pool, he came out from under the bank, gathered his legs under him, and gave a leap that carried him up into the edge of the woods, a little to the left of where the others had entered them. Then he kept right on leaping. He looked like a little green ball bounding along through the trees. And as he bounded, he thought: "I hope P-Peter is in his den, and not off berrying. If he's home, maybe we can head off gug, gug—I mean Garble and rescue Freddy."

It may seem odd that Theodore stuttered even when he was thinking. But he said that he did it on purpose. "You see," he said, "if I don't stutter, then it doesn't sound to me like *me,* and I think maybe it's somebody else thinking, and then I get mixed up. But if I stutter, then I know right away it's my own thought."

A frog can really travel when he gets into the swing of jump—gather your legs—jump—gather your legs—jump. Long before Freddy and his captor had got through the Big Woods, Theodore had reached the bear's den. Luckily Peter was home. Since it was October, it was getting along towards his bedtime, and he was busy airing his blankets and pillows, but he left them hanging on the line and set out at a dead run. Even Theodore was left behind, for although bears look clumsy, they can gallop through the tangle of thick woods faster than you can run on the open road.

And now there were three rescue parties, all headed towards Freddy from different directions. Peter reached him first. He came out of the Big Woods on the north, and there by the side of the old wood road was a station wagon, with the initials H.G. on the door. There was no one in it.

Peter looked at it. "I wonder what these things weigh?" he said. Then he went up to it, and bending down, put his big forepaws under the runningboard. And he was just about to heave the car over on its side when a voice shouted: "Stand away from that car!" and he looked around to see Mr. Garble pointing a pistol at him, while Freddy, with bright steel handcuffs on his fore-trotters, stood dejectedly beside him.

"A pistol!" said Peter. "H'm, that alters things, rather." He got up and walked slowly towards Mr. Garble. "Good morning," he said. "I was just looking—I thought you had a puncture in that rear tire."

"Stand where you are, or your rear tires will get plugged full of punctures," said Mr. Garble menacingly. "Get into the car, pig."

As Freddy obeyed there was a crashing and trampling in the woods, and the Bean animals burst into the open a little way up the road and came galloping down on them.

Of course none of them knew that the pistol wasn't loaded, and as Mr. Garble swung it to cover them while reaching for the doorhandle with his free hand, they skidded to a stop. They stood around him in a semicircle, the cows and

Luckily Peter was home.

goat with horns lowered, the dogs snarling, the cat with back arched and tail three times its natural size—even the placid Hank showed his long wicked teeth.

Nothing is more truly terrifying than the anger of animals. For when an animal snarls, or threatens with horns or claws, you know he just isn't fooling. Freddy knew that in a minute they would rush Mr. Garble in spite of the pistol, and he called to them to stop. "Don't do anything," he said. "You'll only get hurt." Then it occurred to him that, as a pig about to be exiled, perhaps even executed, he was in an even more romantic position than as a lonely wanderer. He forced a brave smile. "Do not weep for me, my friends," he said with simple dignity. "Though I go, never to return, think kindly of me when I am no longer among you. Do not think that I shrink from the fate that awaits me. (Golly," he thought, "that's a good start for a poem.) Tell them," he said,—"tell them that I only did my duty, that—"

The sound of a horn interrupted his last words. Everyone turned to look, and saw the sheriff's car coming up the road.

A look of consternation came over Mr. Garble's face. Now he would have to turn Freddy

over to the sheriff. And the pig knew too much.
No one now was paying any attention to him;
every eye was on the approaching car. Suddenly
he whirled about. "Stop him! Stop thief! He's
trying to escape!" he shouted, and aiming his
pistol at the pig, fired twice.

Mr. Garble would probably have fired again,
but before he could pull the trigger a third
time the sky fell on him. At least that was what
it felt like. What had really happened was that
at the first shot the animals had all turned and
made a dive for him, and there he was with his
face in the dirt and a good half ton of assorted
animals on top of him.

The sheriff's car stopped and he jumped out
and ran up to them. By doing a good deal of
yelling, and by grabbing, now an ear, now a
horn or leg, and pulling hard, he finally got
to the bottom of the heap and dragged Mr. Garble out. Mr. Garble was a mess. He was covered
with dirt and his nose was scratched where it
had been pushed into the road, and he really
did look a lot flatter. He staggered over to the
ditch and threw himself down.

Suddenly somebody said: "Hey, where's
Freddy?" and they all made a rush for the station wagon.

Freddy was lying on his back on the front seat with his eyes closed and his handcuffed fore-trotters folded across his chest. Not having known that the pistol was loaded only with blanks, he quite naturally thought that he was dead, and so he lay as still as possible. He was really very comfortable. "Probably," he thought, "I am now a ghost, and tonight I shall go down and haunt Mr. Garble." And he was thinking of all the different things a ghost could do to make Mr. Garble shake and shiver with fear, when there were a lot of voices around him, and two big paws lifted him up and carried him over to the grass by the roadside.

"That's funny," he thought; "you can't pick up a ghost. Maybe I'm not killed—maybe I'm just mortally wounded." Something wet splashed on his forehead, and he opened one eye to see the faces of all his friends looking down mournfully at him. "Oh, he does look so natural!" murmured Mrs. Wiggins, and another large tear rolled down her broad face to splash on his nose.

He tried to think of something noble to say, something that would be worthy to be quoted among The Last Words of Famous People. Unfortunately he had already made some appropriate and dignified remarks on getting into the car; these, if he said anything more, would become his Next to the Last Words, which would be silly.

However, something had to be said. He dodged another tear, and said to Mrs. Wiggins: "Old partner, we have come to the parting of the ways." He smiled bravely. "We have had good times together, you and I. But at last the hour for me to leave you has struck—" He didn't get any farther, for at that moment the cow burst into loud sobs.

When Mrs. Wiggins cried, she gave it everything she had. You could hear her for miles. The sheriff, who had been chuckling to himself over the act Freddy had been putting on, decided it was time to break it up. But he didn't want to tell them that the pig hadn't been shot at all, because he would be in for a lot of criticism around Centerboro if it got out that he had armed a deputy with a pistol loaded only with blanks. He went over and whacked the pig on the shoulder. "Come on, old partner," he said with a grin. "The hour for you to get up on your hind legs has struck. You aren't wounded; Herb didn't even hit you. Which is a good thing for you, Herb," he said, turning to Mr. Garble, "because law officers that shoot unarmed prisoners usually get put where they can't do any more mischief. Come on, unlock these handcuffs."

Mr. Garble got up with a groan and limped over to the car. "He was trying to escape," he said. But nobody could hear him because Mrs. Wiggins had begun to cry in earnest now, and was making a terrific hullabaloo. The others were trying to explain that Freddy was all right, but she wouldn't listen.

When the handcuffs were off, Freddy sat up and felt himself all over. "No bullet holes?" he said. "My goodness, Mr. Garble is an awful poor shot."

"What?" shouted the sheriff, and Jinx put his mouth close to Freddy's ear. "Go and let Mrs. Wiggins see you," he yelled. "Maybe that will stop her. She'll go on like this for hours if you don't. And it's Sunday, too."

So Freddy went over and stood in front of the cow. After a minute she caught sight of him. She hiccuped twice and then stopped crying.

"I'm all right," he said. "Garble didn't shoot me."

"Freddy!" she said. "You—you're really . . . ?

Oh, how happy that makes me!'' Then her face became sad again. "But how could you let me make such a spectacle of myself? All that about the parting of the ways, and the hour having struck—such dreadfully sad thoughts!'' And she began to cry again.

"Come on, Freddy," said the sheriff. "You're my prisoner now, and I'll have to take you down to the jail." He glanced at Mrs. Wiggins. "She sure is fond of you, Freddy. There ain't any people that would cry like that over me. Not any that could, anyhow."

So Freddy said goodbye to his friends—without any noble phrases this time—and got in the sheriff's car. Even through the noise of the engine they could hear, for quite a long time, the sound of Mrs. Wiggins' grief, as Peter and her two sisters helped her on her homeward way.

That evening Uncle Solomon called at the jail. Freddy and the sheriff were playing checkers when he flew in the window. "Continue your game, gentlemen," he said, perching on the back of a chair. "Don't let me interrupt." And then as the sheriff reached out to move a man: "No, no, sheriff!" he said. "Not that man; oh dear me, no!"

"Eh?" said the sheriff, and he leaned back and studied the board.

"By the way," said Uncle Solomon, "I have been curious about a remark you made to me this morning. About the reason you hadn't gone to church. Your Adam's apple had something to do with it, did it not?"

"Oh," said the sheriff. "Yeah. Why you see, if I go to church, I have to put on a necktie. 'Tain't that I mind; it's sufferin' in a good cause. But I like to sing the hymns. Maybe that's other folks' sufferin'—I don't know. Anyway a hymn starts, say, fairly low. O K, so I'm right with it; so I sing. Then the tune goes up a few notes. Up I go with it, and—well, I expect you ain't got an Adam's apple so you don't know, but the higher the note, the higher your Adam's apple climbs in your throat." He lifted his chin and sang a scale to show them. "Everything's all right so far, but what happens when the tune drops down again? My Adam's apple gets caught on top of my necktie, and my voice stays up with it, and there I am singin' four or five notes higher in the scale than the rest of the congregation, and off the key by that time, like as not. Well, that throws the other singers off, and they begin caterwaulin' in six different keys, and then that throws the organ off, and—well, 'tisn't fittin'. 'Tain't the right kind of noises to be coming out of a church." He leaned forward to move another man.

"Tut, tut!" said the owl sharply, and he drew his hand back again.

So Uncle Solomon thanked him for his explanation, and then turned to Freddy. "My purpose in coming this evening," he said hesitantly, "was—er, to offer you a—" He interrupted himself to stop the sheriff again. "The king, sheriff; the king!"

"If your purpose," said the sheriff with some irritation, "was to finish this game for me, sit down here and finish it!"

"No, no," said the owl. "I beg your pardon; I'm a little upset this evening. No, my purpose —well, in fact I have written a short poem," he said with a titter of embarrassment, "a modest effort, to redeem, in some measure, my shameful neglect of duty this morning."

"Oh, forget it," said Freddy.

"No doubt I shall. Our errors are easily forgotten. However, this poem is in the—the form of a missile—a missive, or epistle, I should say— addressed to you." And he cleared his throat and recited.

"Remarkable pig:

Without ceremonial
May I offer to you this slight testimonial
To your wit and your wisdom, so often ex-
  hibited
On occasions where others are dumb and in-
  hibited.
To your skill metaphorical, brilliance poetical,
Expertness rhetorical, and refinement aestheti-
  cal;
To your sharpness financial, your scope edi-
  torial,
Your feats on the gridiron quite gladiatorial.
And if anyone questions, or has the temerity
To doubt of your honesty, zeal or sincerity,
You have my considered permission to call 'im
  an
Enemy of
  Your good friend,

Uncle Solomon."

And having finished, he gave again the embarrassed titter and flew out of the window.

"Gee whiz!" said the sheriff.

Chapter 14

If you had to go to jail, Freddy thought, there
certainly wasn't a nicer jail to go to than the
Centerboro one. It was just like staying at a
hotel, only it was nicer than a hotel because you
didn't have to pay anything. Of course it was
run differently than most jails. The sheriff let
the prisoners have parties, and go to movies and
ball games because, he said, "I want to turn 'em
into good citizens, and 'tain't any training for
good citizenship if you're locked up in a little
cell all the time with no other citizens to talk
to." The only trouble was that some of the pris-

oners didn't want to leave when their time was up.

The sheriff, however, wouldn't let Freddy have as much freedom as the others had. "Until you've come up for trial and been sentenced, you have to stay right in your cell," he said. "Not more than a month or two, anyway. We'll try to make it as pleasant as we can for you."

"How—how much of a sentence do you think I'll get?" Freddy asked anxiously.

"Oh, five years maybe. Six years. I dunno."

"Six years!" Freddy exclaimed.

"Well," said the sheriff, "you ain't supposed to rob banks, you know."

Freddy was brought up before Judge Willey Monday morning.

"This prisoner, your Honor," said the sheriff, "is accused of robbing the First National Bank of Centerboro of $5000."

"Goodness!" said the judge.

"He respectfully requests," continued the sheriff, "that an early date be set for his trial."

"H'm," said the judge. He took a little calendar from his desk and leafed through it, murmuring to himself. "November . . . have the trial of Mrs. Watson Dickey—husband gave her a box of cigars for Christmas, then smoked 'em himself."

"What did she do?" asked the sheriff curiously.

"Don't know. He disappeared. But there's a strong smell of cigars down cellar . . . H'm, that'll be a long trial . . . Let's see. December? No, have to get Christmas shopping done. Then . . . h'm . . . Mrs. Willey having big Christmas dinner, probably we'll be most of January washing up the dishes. February—" He looked up. "February tenth," he said. "Now is there anyone here who offers bail for the appearance of the prisoner on that date? If so, I set the amount at $5000. No one, eh? I'm not surprised. Sheriff, lock him up."

When they got back to the jail, Freddy said: "This bail business—that means that somebody puts up some money to guarantee that if I'm let out, I'll show up for my trial?"

"That's right," said the sheriff. "And if you don't show up at your trial, they lose the money."

"I guess I stay in jail, then," Freddy said.

Several visitors came to see him on Monday.

The first was Mrs. Bean. "Well, Freddy," she said, "I'm very sorry to see you here. Why, oh why did you do such a thing?"

"I guess you know, ma'am," he said, "why I did it."

"Yes, I guess I do. You think Brother Aaron is an impostor. But that is a matter for me to decide. Oh, Freddy, I know you didn't steal the money for yourself; I know you've hidden it and intend to give it back. Do it now, Freddy, and I can give it to my brother and then my conscience will be clear."

"But he isn't your brother," Freddy insisted.

"Oh, I'd like to shake you!" she exclaimed and her black eyes snapped angrily. Then she relented and put her arms around him and gave him a big hug. "I'm not angry at you," she said, "—not really. But Mr. Bean is. He wouldn't come to see you. And here's another thing for you to think about. Everybody guesses that you've hidden the money somewhere in the woods, and quite a lot of them are up there hunting for it. Suppose they find it and keep it themselves?"

Freddy didn't say anything, and she turned and went out the door. But immediately she put her head back in. "If there's anything you want from the pig pen, I'll have it sent down to you."

So Freddy said he'd like his dictionary and some pencils and paper, and she said all right and went.

Freddy learned from Jinx, who came a little later, that the state troopers were searching for the money. "They just about tore the pig pen to pieces yesterday," he said. "Boy, don't you ever dust the place? They had to keep coming outdoors to sneeze. They even ripped up the cushion in your big chair, and gosh, how they laughed when the cracker crumbs flew! They said they guessed they'd seen untidier places, but they couldn't remember when."

"I suppose they've got a right to search my place," said Freddy, "but I don't see why they have to criticize my housekeeping."

Jinx grinned. "I don't either," he said. "People hadn't ought to criticize you for something you don't do. But there's other people looking for that money, too. Only a lot quieter about it. Herb Garble's one."

"I know," said Freddy. "If somebody happened to see that little package up in the tree— Well, get hold of Uncle Solomon right away, and have him bring the money down here tonight. Don't let the sheriff see him. But the money will be safer here than anywhere else. The sheriff went through my pockets when he brought me in; he won't search me again."

The cat snickered. "First time I ever heard of a thief taking the money he stole right into the jail with him. O K, I'll see to it. Any messages you want to send, just whistle out the window. We're keeping the joint picketed."

Mr. Finnerty and Jason Brewer called that afternoon, and they were pretty mad at Freddy. "You certainly messed up our football season by getting locked up in jail," Jason said. "Here's the Tushville game coming Saturday, and without you we haven't a chance. I guess you've put an end to football in Centerboro all right." But when Freddy had told him the whole story— except where the money was—Jason said: "Well, maybe you did right. But I'd call the game off if I could. We'll be snowed under."

"I thought maybe you could play, if you got out on bail," said Mr. Finnerty. "But I hear the judge set bail at $5000. Nobody's got that kind of money."

Suddenly Freddy thought: "My gracious, I've got it myself! Only of course I can't put it up myself, because they'd know it was Mr.

Bean's and take it away from me. Now, I wonder . . ." He was wondering so hard that he scarcely listened to what Jason and the coach said to him, and after a few minutes, seeing that he wasn't paying any attention to them, they got mad again and left.

As soon as they were gone he went to the window of his cell and looked out. A couple of prisoners were digging dandelions out of the lawn, and behind them a robin was just tugging at one end of an angleworm who didn't seem very anxious to come out of the ground. It was Mrs. Pomeroy. Freddy whistled, and she gave up her argument with the worm, who snapped back into the dirt like a rubber band, and flew up and in between the window bars.

"Hello, Mrs. P," said Freddy. "How's J.J. today?"

"Well he's complaining a lot," she said, "but the wing's doing nicely. I guess the children get on his nerves, that's why he fusses so. Do you want something?"

"See if you can find Mrs. Church, and ask her to come see me tomorrow morning. Tell her to drop in as if she was just paying a call. It's very important."

"I'll get her," said the robin. "If you want

anything while I'm gone, Rabbits Nos. 22 and 18 are over under that bush." And she flew off.

Late that night Uncle Solomon brought the money, and at ten next morning Mrs. Church came. "I brought you an apple pie, Freddy," she said. "But I wouldn't advise you to eat it. It was just an excuse so the sheriff wouldn't know you'd sent for me. I never made a pie before and perhaps I didn't get enough shortening in. The filling's all right, I guess, but the crust—well, maybe you could get into it with a chisel. However," she said, sitting down with the pie in her lap, "let's get down to business. What can I do for you?"

"Well, there is something," said Freddy. "But maybe you won't want to do it, and if you don't, just say so, and—"

"Come on, come on, what is it?" said Mrs. Church with a smile.

"Why, as you may have heard, the judge has set bail for me at $5000."

"And you want me to put it up?" she said. "Gladly, Freddy, gladly. I was wondering about that this morning, but—"

"Oh, no! Please!" Freddy interrupted. "I don't want you to put up any of your money. You might lose it. If Mr. Garble catches me

Late that night Uncle Solomon brought the money.

and ships me off, you'd never get it back. No," he said bringing out the package of money and handing it to her, "here's the money that belongs to Mr. Bean. If you are willing you can take that to Judge Willey and put it up as my bail. I only want to get out so I can play in the game Saturday, and not let the team down. If I do get captured, you won't lose anything. And the money will go back to Mr. Bean."

Mrs. Church laughed so hard that the pie bounced off her lap on to the floor. "You're a caution, Freddy! You rob a bank and then when the police catch you, instead of giving up the money, you use it to bail yourself out. And yet, I don't know. Right now I'm in possession of stolen goods," she said, holding up the package, "and if I hide it or use it to bail you out, that makes me a confederate of the robber. I don't know much about law, but I know that if anyone found it out, they could put me right in the next cell."

"My goodness," said Freddy, "I didn't think —here, give it back. Of course you mustn't do it."

"On the other hand," Mrs. Church went on, putting the money in her purse, "I'm on your side, Freddy. You can't keep the money here.

And if I keep it for you, I might just as well put it up as bail. Furthermore, if we *are* caught, and Judge Willey, who is my cousin, sentences me to prison, I'll never let him hear the last of it!

"And so," she said, getting up, "I'd better take care of it right away."

Freddy argued, but her mind was made up. "You leave it to me," she said. "And when the sheriff turns you loose, better come up to my house. I don't suppose you'll want to go back to the farm."

When she had gone, Freddy picked up the pie. The fall hadn't hurt it; even the edge where it had struck the floor was undamaged. He poked at the crust, but it was as hard as wood. He looked at it a minute, then he took it out into the dining room and put it up on the plate rail, between two of the valuable plates of the sheriff's collection of rare china.

Chapter 15

As soon as Freddy was released on bail, he put the pie under one arm and his dictionary under the other and went up to Mrs. Church's.

She laughed when she saw the pie. "I don't know what you can do with it," she said. "It might make a nice cornerstone for a house."

"Well," said Freddy; "one thing about it: it'll be just as good in five years, and maybe I'll be hungry when I get out of prison."

Freddy spent that evening with his dictionary open at the list of Common English Christian Names, in the back. He was sure that Mr.

Doty's real initials were the ones on his trunk, and while the B might stand for any one of a thousand last names, the chances were that the C stood for one of the commoner names beginning with that letter. So he made a list of the commoner ones. He discarded the one which the dictionary list started off with—Cadwallader, however, and used his own judgment about Constantine and Cuthbert and Caesar. "If they're common Christian names," he thought, "that dictionary man, Mr. Webster, —well, I wonder what he'd call an unusual name?" He got a list of eight names, and decided to try those.

The next afternoon he reported for football practice. Everybody was glad, for now there was a good chance of beating Tushville Saturday, and as word that he was back on the team got around, many people closed their offices and stores early and came up to watch. Practice was just about over when Mr. Gridley and Mr. Garble appeared.

They walked right out on the field, and Mr. Garble shouted: "Stop! I protest against allowing this pig to be a member of the school team. I represent the School Board, and I have called upon Mr. Gridley to order the coach to dismiss him. He is well known as a hardened criminal, a bank robber, who should not be allowed to consort with our innocent children. Mr. Gridley, do your duty!"

There was a good deal of angry muttering from the townspeople who had been watching from the sidelines, and one of the boys on the team said: "Ah, why don't you mind your own business!"

Mr. Gridley looked rather unhappy. "I am afraid, Mr. Finnerty," he said, "that I have no choice. Since the School Board orders it—"

A precise, sarcastic little laugh made him stop and look up. Uncle Solomon was perched on the crossbar of the goalposts.

"One moment," said the owl. "I am not a member of your distinguished Board, but as a close friend and admirer of the accused, may I be permitted to ask a question?"

Although small, the owl spoke with such dignity that Mr. Gridley said: "Why, of course," but Mr. Garble said angrily: "Oh, yeah? Well, I'm not going to answer questions by any little snake-eating squawk-owl!"

"Dear me," said Uncle Solomon with a titter, "I fail to see what remarks on my personal habits have to do with what we were discussing.

Would you care to explain the connection, Mr. Garble?"

"Yah!" said Mr. Garble disgustedly.

"Thank you," said Uncle Solomon. "And, Mr. Gridley, since that seems to be the sum total of Mr. Garble's argument, I suggest we simply drop the whole thing."

Mr. Garble had turned his back on the owl. "Mr. Gridley, do your duty," he ordered.

But again the maddening titter interrupted him. "May I point out," said the owl, "that I have not yet asked my question?"

Mr. Garble was beside himself with rage— and you can't blame him much, for there is no sound so insulting as the laugh of a screech owl. He pulled out his pistol and pointed it at Uncle Solomon. "For two cents—" he began.

"I haven't the sum on me at the moment," said the owl calmly. "But knowing your light-fingered ways with money which does not belong to you, I am not surprised at your trying to chisel even two cents out of me. I permit myself this personal comment," he remarked to Mr. Gridley, "only because Mr. Garble has seen fit to make similar comments about me." Then he turned back to Mr. Garble. "However, if one of the boys will advance me the two cents, I will gladly give it to you. Particularly as I do not believe that you could hit a barn, even if you were inside it. Well, dear me," he said, as Mr. Garble hesitated; "go ahead!"

And Mr. Garble, stung to a fury of rage, pulled the trigger.

Uncle Solomon had learned from the sheriff that the gun was loaded only with blanks. But before Mr. Garble could shoot again, a heavy hand fell on the back of his neck, and the sheriff said: "I've spoken to you about that pistol before. If you let that thing off just once more, Herb, I'll pull your ears back and tie 'em in a bow knot behind your head. Now go ahead, owl; what's your question?"

"Evidently, Mr. Garble," said Uncle Solomon, "you are no more skillful with a gun than you are with an argument. However—have you any proof of your accusation that this pig is a hardened criminal?"

"Everybody knows it," said Mr. Garble sulkily.

"*I* do not know it. However, if such an accusation is a reason for his being dismissed from the team, I hereby accuse you of attempted

Mr. Garble pulled the trigger.

murder, and I demand that you be thrown off
the School Board.''

Mr. Garble gritted his teeth, but with the
sheriff's hand still on his neck, all he said was:
''You're just trying to mix me up. I say this pig
is a thief, and he ought not to be in the school,
much less on the team.''

''I am afraid that you are trying to mix *me*
up now,'' said Uncle Solomon. ''Your saying he
is a thief doesn't make him one. Furthermore,
since he has not confessed to any crime, nor yet
been tried and found guilty . . . Well, dear
me, I think I see one among the audience here
who is not only a member of the School Board,
but also a distinguished jurist. Judge Willey,
would you be good enough to step forward and
give us a ruling on this perplexing matter?''

So the judge came forward. ''My learned
friend,'' he said with a bow to the owl, ''has, I
think, clearly shown the unsoundness of Mr.
Garble's position. Under our laws in America,
Mr. Garble, the laws of a free people, every person is considered innocent until he is proved
guilty. The School Board, therefore, *must* consider this pig innocent. Furthermore, Mr. Garble, should we dismiss him from the team because of your assertion that he is a criminal, he

could then bring suit against you for slander, defamation of character, perjury, conspiracy and bad temper. And if the case were to come up before me, I should unhesitatingly award him damages running into very high figures indeed, which you would have to pay. I think," he said, turning with a bow to Uncle Solomon, "that that is an opinion in which my learned friend will heartily concur."

The owl returned the bow. "With the utmost completeness," he said. "You have given us, my esteemed colleague, an exposition of the finer points of the legal aspects of this case which, for clarity, brevity and wit, it would be difficult to equal in the highest courts in the land."

They bowed again to each other and then looked sternly at Mr. Garble. And Mr. Garble growled angrily and walked off the field.

After the practice Freddy went back to Mrs. Church's. He found his hostess sitting on the porch. "The funniest thing, Freddy," she said. "You know that terrible pie I brought you?— well, I've found out why it was so hard. You know, after my cook left, I wondered why some of the things I made turned out so queer. But that cook was a very odd person. I don't think she could read, for she kept everything in the wrong place. The sugar was in the salt jar, and the coffee was in a tin marked baking soda, and so on. So when I made the pie, I used what I supposed was flour. But do you know what she had in the flour bin?—plaster of Paris!"

"That was sort of dangerous, wasn't it?" said Freddy.

"I guess it was! But what I wanted to tell you was, I've baked another pie just like it, except the filling is different. —Oh, don't look so thunderstruck; I'll tell you why. Sit down.

"You see," she said, "I didn't use Mr. Bean's money to bail you out. The more I thought of it, the more I thought it was a bad idea. I used my own money. And the money you gave me—well, I baked it in that pie."

"But—but how will we ever get it out?"

"When the time comes you can crack it open with a sledge hammer. In the meantime, it's safe. Nobody but an alligator could take a bite out of it. Now what did you do with the other one?"

Freddy told her. "And I think tonight I'll take this one down and substitute it for the other. After all, it's stolen money, and it isn't right for you to have it here."

"I don't mind," she said. "But the jail is an

awfully good place for it. If you can do it without making the sheriff suspicious. You can go down after supper."

"After—supper?" Freddy looked at her doubtfully. "Er—what are we going to have for supper?"

She laughed. "Don't worry. Everything's in the right place now. I won't give you ammonia soup or anything like that."

So after supper Freddy went down to the jail with the money pie under his coat. The sheriff was playing checkers with Looey, and he didn't pay any attention when Freddy wandered out into the dining room, and he only said: "So long; drop in again," when Freddy came back and said he guessed he'd go home.

Freddy really did go home: he went out to the farm. On his way he threw the apple pie into some bushes, where it was found the next spring by some Boy Scouts. It looked good, and they sat down by the road to eat it. Half an hour and three broken teeth later they threw it back where they'd found it, and I guess it's there yet.

Freddy sneaked into the cow barn. He didn't wake Mrs. Wiggins up at once, because he wanted to try out the idea he had for getting rid of Mr. Doty. He crept up close to her and whispered: "Hey, Mrs. Johnson!"

Mrs. Wiggins went right on sleeping.

"Hey, Mrs. Prendergast," Freddy whispered.

Mrs. Wiggins went on sleeping.

"Hey, Mrs. Peppercorn!"

No response.

Then Freddy said in the same tone: "Hey, Mrs. Wiggins!" And the cow raised her head and said: "What? What is it?"

"It's me—Freddy," said the pig. "Quiet! I don't want the Beans to hear me."

And then he told her his idea. "You see, you didn't wake up till I used your own name. And that same way we can find out Mr. Doty's name."

Mrs. Wiggins didn't see what good that would do.

"It will do this much," said Freddy, "that if he wakes up hearing somebody whispering his real name in the night,—well, who would know his name around here? Only Garble."

"Land sakes, what would Mr. Garble be doing in Mrs. Bean's spare room in the middle of the night?"

"That's just the point," Freddy said, and he went on and told her his plan.

" 'Twon't work," said Mrs. Wiggins. "How

you going to get into Doty's room? And if you do, and he wakes up—there's enough light in that room at night to recognize you by."

"Of course I can't get in there," said Freddy. "The one to do it is Mr. Webb. He can spin down next to Doty's ear, and then if he whispers, Doty won't see him, and—oh, I've worked that all out. But there's no rush. If you'll talk to Webb in the morning, then I'll meet him in a day or two and fix it all up."

"Yes, you don't want to stay around here. Mr. Bean is awful mad at you. All right, I'll speak to Webb. And you know, Freddy," she said, "you could work the same thing on Mr. Garble."

"Golly," said Freddy excitedly, "that's right. Sure we could! Oh, we've got to think this over carefully. Is Mr. Bean so mad at me that he won't let you come down to the game Saturday?"

Mrs. Wiggins chuckled. "I don't know as he's quite as mad as that. I wouldn't be surprised if he came down himself. The way I look at it, Freddy, there's only half of him that's mad at you—the half that don't like your pretending to be him on the telephone, and running off with his money. But there's another half that's kind of doubtful about Doty. He's not nearly so sure Doty is who he claims he is as Mrs. Bean is. Gracious, I'm too sleepy to talk—getting my verbs all mixed up.''

"Well, goodnight,'' said Freddy, and got on his bicycle and rode back down to his comfortable room at Mrs. Church's.

Chapter 16

The crowd that streamed out to the athletic field that Saturday to see Centerboro play Tushville was one of the largest in the history of the team. Main Street was deserted; indeed the only person left in the village was old Mr. Lawrence, who had gone out the previous Saturday, under the impression that that was the day of the game, and was so mad about his mistake that he stayed home.

Most of Tushville had come over too, for they had heard about the pig on the Centerboro team and had laughed themselves sick over it. But the players, who knew how Freddy had upset Plutarch Mills, hadn't laughed. "If that pig tries any of his funny business on *us,*" they said, "we'll sizzle his bacon for him!" And when the two teams came out to warm up, Freddy was scared. He was sure that a procession of ants with very cold feet was promenading up his backbone and he could feel that his tail had come uncurled. For the Tushvillers were big. Even those who were plainly schoolboys were big, but the right guard and the right tackle, who would be facing him, were grown men and one of the backs had a black beard.

"I want you to hold back during the first quarter, Freddy," said Mr. Finnerty. "You'll have to play hard, of course, but don't get through their line too fast, and when you block, act sort of clumsy, so they'll get the idea you can't do them much harm. We'll try to get them off guard, so that when you really do go in we can give them the works. Jason, you better play a passing game at first, and let Jimmy Witherspoon punt as early as the second down. O K, I guess we're ready."

Centerboro kicked off, and Black Beard caught it and came pounding down the field behind four of his team mates. The Centerboro players converged upon him, but Freddy hung back, trotting now this way and now that, as if bewildered. Angry voices from the home fans shouted at him: "Come on, pig! Get in there and play! What are you doing—looking for four-leaf clovers?" But Freddy paid no attention. When Black Beard was finally pulled down on Centerboro's thirty-yard line, he was off at the other side of the field.

The angry yells went on, but they were drowned out in a shout of laughter from the Tushville supporters. The Tushville principal, a big red-faced man, came over and slapped Mr. Gridley on the back. "So that's your famous pig!" he jeered. "You better put a fence around the field to keep him from getting lost!"

Mr. Gridley just shrugged his shoulders and moved off.

Tushville went into a huddle, and then snapped into position. The tackle opposite Freddy was a giant who scowled ferociously at him. "Know my name, pig?" he growled. "It's Joe Butcher. Butcher—get that? I'm the butcher and you're the pig, and, boy, are you on the chopping block now!"

"Oh, dear!" said Freddy. "Oh, dear!" And he pretended to shiver. For he wasn't scared any longer. "If this guy is trying to scare me," he thought, "it must mean that he's scared himself. Though why he should be, after that last play, I don't know." So when the center passed the ball, he crouched low, and as Butcher came at him he sprang and drove his snout right into the man's stomach.

A pig's snout is pretty tough. Mr. Butcher said Whoosh! and doubled up on the ground. But the play, a sweep around left end, went on and Tushville scored a touchdown.

While they were waiting for Butcher to get his wind back, Jason said: "Take it easy, Freddy. Mr. Finnerty said never mind if they score."

Tushville kicked off, and Clip Brannigan, who played right end, got the ball and managed to reach the middle of the field before he was downed. Then Jimmy Witherspoon dropped back and punted. It was a beautiful punt, and a Tushville back fell on it on his ten-yard line.

When they took position for the next play, Butcher didn't make any more faces at Freddy. But he looked pretty determined as he crouched, with one hand protecting his stomach, and the other on the ground. "I mustn't let him take me too seriously yet," Freddy thought; so when the ball was passed and Butcher plunged at him, he just turned and ran away. He circled round to the right, and then he saw that Black Beard was in the clear, only a few yards from him, and just catching a long pass. It looked like a sure touchdown, for as the man started to run there wasn't a Centerboro player anywhere near him. Except Freddy.

Freddy knew that he ought to hold back, and yet he didn't want that touchdown made. Black Beard was running straight towards him. He was grinning and evidently quite sure that Freddy couldn't stop him. So Freddy didn't try to tackle. As the man came on, he squealed despairingly, and then zigzagged, as if trying to dodge. "Out of my way, old lard bucket!" Black Beard said. And then Freddy, as if completely demoralized, threw himself down on the ground. But as he fell, he rolled. He rolled right into Black Beard's legs. And Black Beard turned an elegant cartwheel, dropped the ball, and ended, very much perplexed, lying flat on his back.

The ball bounded off to one side and Jason fell on it, and the entire crowd, Tushvillers and Centerboroites alike, burst into yells of laughter.

Again Centerboro punted, and the game went on. The Tushville team felt sure of winning; they had lost any anxiety they might have had about the much-talked-of pig, who was evidently half scared to death; and they took things fairly easy. At the end of the quarter they had scored another touchdown, and led, 14–0.

With the game apparently already won, Tushville played carelessly at the beginning of the second quarter, and nobody bothered much about Freddy. They had made several plays from a single wingback formation, pulling Butcher over to the other side of the line, and they were so sure that Freddy couldn't do anything that they scarcely bothered to block him. Again they shifted in the same way and then Jason gave Freddy a nod. "I'll be right behind you," he said.

The instant the ball was passed Freddy was through the line. There was no opposition. Black Beard had the ball and was just about to throw a long pass when the pig hit him. He went into the air as if he had stepped on a land mine, the ball popped up, and Jason, who was right behind the pig, caught it before it touched the ground and ran down the open field for a touchdown.

He went into the air as if he had stepped on a land mine.

At first the Tushvillers thought that had been merely a lucky break for Centerboro. But when, on the next kick-off, Freddy tore down the field under the ball, looking like a small charging buffalo in his headgear and padded jersey, and knocked over Johnny Gibbs just as he had caught the ball, they began to take notice. First they shifted tackles, replacing Butcher, who was now permanently breathless from having been butted in the stomach a second time—with a boy named Clint. Then when Clint seemed unable to hold the pig, they began to gang up on Freddy.

But it isn't easy to gang up on an active pig, as any farmer knows. He is fast and tricky, and it is practically impossible to get hold of him. Freddy was through on every Tushville play, and when Centerboro had the ball, he could knock a tackler off his feet and be off after another one almost before the first man had hit the ground. In that quarter Centerboro made three touchdowns. The score was Tushville 21, Centerboro 20.

There were three ringers on the Tushville team: Butcher, Black Beard, and a hard-faced tough named Canner. And at the beginning of the next quarter it became plain to Freddy that the three had decided, by fair means or foul, to put him out of the game. In the scrimmages, when they thought the referee couldn't see, they slugged and kicked him; once Canner got hold of his tail and twisted it till he squealed. Frequently, of course, the referee saw them and each time it cost Tushville fifteen yards for unnecessary roughness. After that they were more careful, for the Tushville captain had to keep calling them down too. But they kept right on.

The crowd on the Centerboro side was getting mad about it. They jeered the ringers and threatened them, and once, when Canner kicked Freddy in plain sight of everybody, they poured right out on to the field and surrounded him, shouting menacingly, and old Mrs. Peppercorn flew at the bully and whacked him over the head with her umbrella. I don't know why she had it with her, but it was nice that she did.

The game might have broken up right there in a free-for-all fight, for the Tushvillers were moving down towards them, and Mr. Gridley and the Tushville principal were shaking their fists at each other. But Freddy and Jason and Mr. Finnerty managed to get them to listen. And then Mr. Finnerty said: "Ladies and gentlemen, please go back to your places. We want to win this game, and we know we can. We know Tushville has three men who have no business on any school team. But we're going to show them that that kind of dishonest football doesn't pay off. We're going to force Tushville to play clean football after this, and we're going to do it by giving them an almighty licking."

"That's all very well," said Judge Willey angrily, "but how about Freddy?"

Freddy was now mad clean through. He had no grudge against the regular Tushville players, but he had a good big one against the three ringers, who stood there with sneering smiles on their faces. "I'm all right, Judge," he said. "I'm going to get these boys to apologize to me after the game."

Butcher laughed right out at that, but the judge and the sheriff looked at each other and winked. They both knew something about pigs.

Centerboro had the ball, and the team went into a huddle. "Try some straight line drives, Jason," said Freddy. "You don't have to worry about me. If those ringers want to rough it up, I can play rough too."

"All right," said Jason. "We might start off with your plough play."

The plough play was one that they had developed in practice, and depended on Freddy's ability to upset, and really plough up, the whole opposing line. When Jason called the signal the Centerboro line, instead of plunging forward, sprang back and swung around right end ahead of the ball carrier. This left the men in the Tushville line suddenly with no opposition, and off balance, and it was then that Freddy, instead of shoving through, turned right, and with his snout close to the ground drove right down the enemy's line, upsetting in succession their right guard, center, left guard and left tackle. The first time he got clear through and joined the sweep around end, which gained forty yards.

Then it was first down on Tushville's fifteen-yard line. Freddy mixed up the line all right, and Clip Brannigan got around for a touchdown. But Freddy had been stopped, and a number of players had piled up on him—among them, Black Beard, who gave him several short arm jabs in the stomach. But Freddy had had enough of that. He twisted around and bit Black Beard in the leg. The man let out a screech, and at the same minute the whistle blew for the end of the quarter.

A pig can give a terrible bite. Freddy could probably have taken a piece right out of his tormenter's leg; as it was, he crunched down pretty hard. Black Beard got up slowly and limped over to the referee. "He bit me!" he yelled. "That pig bit me!"

The referee had had about enough, too. He looked at the man coldly. "Yeah?" he said. "Why didn't you bite him back?" And walked away.

The Centerboro crowd had gone wild with delight. They cheered Clip and they cheered Freddy, and they gave three long boos for Black Beard. "What grade you in, whiskers?" they yelled. "Can you spell 'cat'?" "Did he hurt his wittle leg? Let Freddy kiss it and make it well." Some of the Tushvillers shouted for Freddy to be taken out of the game, but there were others who really didn't care for the brand of football their team played, and there was a lot of arguing and one or two small fights.

Black Beard limped around, glaring at Freddy until Butcher and Canner came over and helped him off the field. They were whispering together, and evidently planning to get back at Freddy; but he was too mad to care. "Don't worry, Freddy," Mr. Finnerty said.

"The referee's watching them. And I don't think he'll watch you too carefully. We're 27 to 21 now; let's go in and give them the works, boys."

So Centerboro did. They had been holding back one play, and now they tried it. Freddy couldn't carry a ball, but he figured that if he slipped his headgear down so that it hung under his chin, somebody could shove the ball into it and the chances were, the first time at least, that Tushville would never notice him until he was over the goal line. And that was just what happened. He dropped back, pulled the headgear down, and when Jason pushed the ball into it, he ran right around left end for a touchdown without being intercepted.

Of course Tushville complained and there was a huddle over the rule book, but there didn't seem to be any rule covering just that play, and the touchdown stood. A little later he tried it again, but this time he was caught. He knocked over Johnny Gibbs, but Canner fell on him, and then Butcher, and Black Beard piled on top. And they all began punching him. "Soak him, boys," Butcher muttered. "We can put him out of the game if the referee won't."

Now down at the end of the field was the

buggy, with Hank hitched up to it, and the Beans and Mr. Doty sitting in it. Right up to the last minute Mr. Bean had said that he wouldn't go to the game. "That pig," he growled—"I've disowned him. He ain't one of my animals any more. I'm not interested in anything he does."

"Unless he returns the money, Mr. B.," Mrs. Bean put in.

"Nope," said Mr. Bean firmly. "I don't ask my animals to agree with me in everything. But I do expect 'em to be ruled by my decisions. He set his judgment up against me, and acted on it. You can't run a farm that way."

"Well, land of Goshen, Mr. B.," Mrs. Bean said, "you ain't running a farm when you go to a football game."

But Mr. Bean still said no.

But about an hour before the time the game was scheduled to begin, Mr. Bean came into the house. "Well," he said testily, "ain't you got a hat on? Expect me to wait all day?"

"Well, well," said Mr. Doty, looking out of the window, "you got Hank harnessed up to the buggy."

Mrs. Bean didn't say anything. She didn't even smile, though she probably wanted to. She hurried up and got her hat on, and they went out and climbed into the buggy.

Freddy had been too busy to pay much attention to the crowd, and Mr. Bean had pulled up Hank some distance back of the goal posts. "Hank's kind of skittish—don't want to get too close to all the wavin' and bellerin'," he said in explanation. Mrs. Bean didn't say anything. She knew that he didn't want people to know that he had come to watch Freddy play.

When the three ringers got Freddy down and started to pummel him, the referee started for them. But the fight was over before he got there. For Freddy knew what he was in for. The three had figured out that they would get their revenge by beating him up, and then the referee would call the game off and Tushville would claim that it had not really been defeated at all. So he went into violent action. He squirmed out from under them, biting and snapping. He tore off Black Beard's jersey, gave a good crunch on Butcher's thumb, and took the seat out of Canner's pants, in about three seconds. But once clear of them, he didn't run; he whirled and went at them again. They couldn't get up, for as soon as one of them got to his knees Freddy would either butt him in the stomach, or grab an arm or leg and pull him down again. The crowd streamed out and formed a circle around them, but no one dared to try to separate them.

Far up the field, Mr. Bean couldn't see very well what went on. He stood up in the buggy and peered down towards the crowd. All at once he grabbed the whip out of the socket. "They've got Freddy down! Go on, Hank!" he shouted. And the old white horse, as determined as Mr. Bean to dash to the rescue, started. He swung from a trot into a gallop, and down the field they swept, with Mr. Bean standing up and waving his whip, and Mrs. Bean and Mr. Doty hanging on for dear life. Mrs. Church said afterwards that if the chariot races in the Roman forum were anything like that, she wished she had been born a thousand years earlier.

The crowd scrambled to get clear as the buggy dashed up. Mr. Bean jumped out with the whip in his hand. "Get away from my pig, you tarnation rascals!" he shouted.

"You get him away from *us!*" wailed Black Beard, then gave a yelp as Freddy nipped him in the side.

Indeed the ringers were all through. They rolled and crawled to get away, but Freddy herded them together, distributing nips to any surfaces that seemed to invite them. But when he saw Mr. Bean he left them and went over to the buggy.

"Oh, Mr. Bean," he said, "did I hear you say that I was your pig? I—I thought you'd disowned me."

Mr. Bean frowned. "I have. 'Tain't you I'm helping, and don't you think it! Would have done the same for any animal. I won't see even a centipede abused." And though obviously none of the three men was at the moment doing anything but trying to get away as quickly as possible, he gave a few cuts at their calves with his whip. Then he got back in, looking rather embarrassed, and shook the reins. "Giddap, Hank," he said, and drove off.

In the meantime the captains and the referees had held a conference. Tushville had demanded that Freddy be taken out. "You take out your three ringers and we'll take out the pig," said Centerboro. And at last it was decided that way. The teams, now evenly matched, now held each other without scoring. But the final score was Centerboro 40, Tushville 21.

While he was sitting on the sidelines, watching, Freddy saw Canner coming towards him, and he braced himself to jump. But the man was holding out his hand. "You sure can take it, pig," he said, "and you can dish it out in lumps, too. You said you were going to make us apologize, and I'm one that's doing it right now. Those other boys—" He shook hands with Freddy and dropped down beside him. "They ain't very good sports," he said lowering his voice, "and I'll give you a tip. They're cooking up something for the next game—when is it, two weeks?"

"You mean you're not sore at me?" Freddy asked.

"What for? I got no business playing here on a school team. It's pretty cheap stuff and I'm through with it." He got up as the whistle blew. "Game's over," he said. "So long, pig; I'll be seeing you." And as the cheering Centerboro crowd made for Freddy and Jason and swung them up on their shoulders, he waved his hand and walked off the field.

Chapter 17

It was midnight and Mr. and Mrs. Webb were sitting on the ceiling of the Beans' spare room. They were sitting upside down, but that is no trick for a spider—indeed it is much more pleasant, because it takes the weight off your body and makes you feel very light and comfortable. Just try it some time.

Below them in the bed Mr. Doty was sleeping peacefully.

"Well, father," said Mrs. Webb, "he's settled down now for good. Better do your stuff, my pet." She had picked up some rather deplorable phrases in Hollywood.

So Mr. Webb spun down on a long strand until he was just an inch above Mr. Doty's left ear. "Hey, Charlie!" he whispered.

Mr. Doty kept right on breathing peacefully in and out.

"Hey, Chester!"

Nothing happened.

"Hey, Clint! . . . Hey, Clifford! . . . Hey, Clarence!"

At the name "Clarence," Mr. Doty stirred and raised up on one elbow. "What is it?" he whispered.

"Pssst!" said Mr. Webb. "Don't move; just listen. The Beans are awake. I'm Garble. I'm over at the window."

"What's the matter—something gone wrong?" Mr. Doty asked.

"You better believe something's gone wrong! The sheriff knows who you are—he's got your jail record, and he's coming out to tell the Beans in the morning."

This was a long chance to take—mentioning a jail record. But Freddy had remembered how scared Mr. Doty had been to go near the jail, and he felt pretty sure that the man had been in jail at some time in the past. And it certainly worked. Mr. Doty sat right up. "Hey, that's bad!" he said, and put his feet out of bed.

He didn't question that it was Mr. Garble speaking, for no one else would have known his first name, and all voices sound alike when they whisper. But when he sat up he moved far enough away from the spider so that he could no longer hear the whisper. And Mr. Webb, swinging at the end of his strand, couldn't get any closer.

Mrs. Webb's brain was no bigger than the head of a pin but it was a good one. If Mr. Doty went to the window and saw that there was no Mr. Garble there, their trick would fail. She hustled across the ceiling until she was directly above Mr. Doty, and then spun down quickly until she was by his ear. "Don't move!" she warned him. "I think old Bean's listening outside your door. Look, Clarence, our scheme's blown up. They know all about you—and I mean *all!*"

"You mean that Watertown job last year?" said Mr. Doty.

"Yes. But even without that they can prove that you're pretending to be Doty in order to get his money. You know what that means."

Mr. Doty didn't say anything for a minute. Then very cautiously he crept out of bed and over to the window. He knelt there and said in a whisper: "I'm broke, Herb; I got enough gas to get me back to Oswego, but you'd better send me some money there if you don't want me to give the sheriff the whole story. And don't forget that address: 24 Killington Street."

He leaned slowly out of the window. "Hey, Herb," he whispered, "where in blazes are you?" He looked up at the eaves and down at the ground, then after a minute pulled his head in. "I wonder," he muttered. Then he shook his head. "Can't take any chances." He listened for a moment at the door, examined the locks on his trunk with a flashlight, then began quietly throwing things into a small bag.

To Charles' astonishment when he came out of the henhouse next morning there was Mr. Doty getting into his car. Mr. Bean's head, in its red and white nightcap, was sticking out of the window, and Mr. Bean's voice was demanding sleepily what in tarnation Mr. Doty was up to.

"Well, well," said Mr. Doty, "didn't want to disturb you, William. Got to go down to Wash-

ington for a day or two. Can't tell you about it
—secret mission for the F.B.I. Back in a day or
two." The car started with a roar and tore down
the driveway.

"Huh!" said Charles crossly. "And here's
Freddy, too. What's the use my crowing if
they're all going to get up in the middle of the
night?" But he crowed anyway.

Mr. Bean, too, had caught sight of Freddy.
"What are you doing here?" he demanded.
"Didn't I tell you you don't live here any
more?"

"Now, Mr. B." Mrs. Bean's head appeared
beside her husband's. "Where's Brother Aaron
off to?"

"I think he's gone away for good," said
Freddy. "But I can tell you more about it when
I've had a talk with the spiders."

"Talk with spiders!" Mr. Bean repeated disgustedly. "Well, you go talk with your spiders
on somebody else's property. I'm going to get
dressed." Their heads disappeared.

Later, however, Mrs. Bean came out to the
pig pen. "Freddy," she said, "what did you
mean? What have the spiders got to do with
Brother Aaron?"

So Freddy told her.

"But I—I just can't believe it!" she said. "I . . . Why, he left his trunk!"

"You can send it to 24 Killington Street, Oswego, I guess he'll get it."

She looked pretty upset. "I can't believe it!" she repeated. "You must be wrong, Freddy."

"No. His name is Clarence something, and not Aaron Doty at all. He's someone Mr. Garble sent for, someone he knew before. To get the money. But it's easy to prove it." And when he had told her how, after thinking it over, she agreed to try it.

So Mrs. Bean went into the house and called Mr. Garble on the phone. "Mr. Garble? This is Mrs. Skuznik, at Dutch Flats. A man just drove in here and asked me to phone you. Said he didn't have time to call you himself. Said to tell you Clarence says to come right out. It's important." And before he could ask any questions she hung up. "But I still don't see why he'd come," she said.

"Maybe he won't. But if he does, it will be because he knows Mr. Doty is Clarence, won't it?"

"I suppose so," said Mrs. Bean with a worried frown. "Oh, if he does come, I'll—well, I'll find out." So Freddy went back outside.

Sure enough, breakfast wasn't yet on the table when a car drove into the yard and Mr. Garble got out and tapped on the door. "Good morning, Mrs. Bean," he said cheerily. "Mr. Doty around? I had to come out this way early, and I thought I'd drop in and just give him this book I promised to lend him."

"Come in, Mr. Garble; come in," said Mrs. Bean.

So he went in and sat down. Mr. Bean was sitting by the window. "Morning, Herb," he said, and that was all he said, for he had promised Mrs. Bean not to interfere.

"Lovely morning," said Mr. Garble.

"Beautiful," said Mrs. Bean. "I suppose that's why Clarence decided to drive back to Oswego today. You can forward the book to him there. Let's see—24 Killington Street, I think was the address he left."

At the name "Clarence" Mr. Garble leaped in his chair as if he had been stung by six hornets, all at once. "C-Clarence?" he said. "Who's Clarence?" But his lips were so stiff that he could hardly get the words out.

Mrs. Bean knew then that Freddy had been right. She got up and stood over Mr. Garble. "I'll tell you," she said quietly. "He's the man you got to come up here and pretend to be my brother. He's the impostor who very nearly ruined us, because I couldn't believe that anyone would practice such a wicked deception. We know the whole story."

"But you can't prove anything!" Mr. Garble stammered. He had got up and was edging towards the door. "You can't do anything to me. I didn't have a thing to do with his coming here; I'm not responsible—"

He stopped, for Mr. Bean had got up, and Mr. Bean's hand had taken him by the arm. "That's right, Herb," Mr. Bean said. "You're as innocent as a little woolly lamb." He patted him kindly on the head. Then suddenly his manner changed. "Get out!" he roared, and with one hand he flung open the door, with the other he rushed Mr. Garble outside, and then with one large capable boot he kicked Mr. Garble right out into the middle of the barnyard, and with the other large capable boot he kicked the door shut.

"Boy, what a beautiful punt!" Freddy exclaimed as he saw Mr. Garble fly through the air.

Inside the house Mr. Bean rubbed his hands. "My," he said with a broad grin which was visible even through his whiskers, "that's given me quite an appetite. Mrs. B., let's have breakfast!"

So they ate a big breakfast, and then Mr. Bean filled his pipe for the first time in weeks, and lit it. But he had hardly taken two puffs when he laid it down again. "That money," he said. Then he went out to the pig pen.

Freddy was waiting. He looked at Mr. Bean and Mr. Bean looked at him. Freddy looked scared, but if there was any expression on Mr. Bean's face, Freddy couldn't see it, for both face and expression were behind Mr. Bean's whiskers.

After a minute Mr. Bean said: "I suppose you want to come back here to live after you get out of prison? Well, if a prison term has taught you a lesson, I guess you can."

"Why—thanks, Mr. Bean," Freddy said. "But I didn't really steal the money. I know where it is. I'm going to get it now. They won't send me to jail for that."

"Giving back what you stole don't wipe out your stealin' it," said Mr. Bean. "Once you get tangled up with the law, 'tain't so easy to get untangled again. You've got to stand trial. I couldn't stop that if I wanted to."

"Oh," said Freddy. Then he said: "I don't

care." And after a minute he said: "I'll get the money."

"I'll go with you," said Mr. Bean. So he harnessed Hank and they drove down to the jail.

The sheriff was surprised to hear that the stolen money was hidden right in his jail. And he was more surprised when Freddy led the way to the dining-room and told them it was hidden there.

"It was a fool place to hide it, Freddy," he said. "Right in a nest of burglars, as you might say."

"Blamedest, silliest thing I ever heard of!" said Mr. Bean.

"All right, sheriff," said Freddy, "if you don't think it was safe, you find it."

"That ain't hard," said the sheriff. So he hunted. He went through the sideboard, and he looked in the cupboards and under the carpet and in the sugar bowls. " 'Tain't here," he said at last.

Freddy would have liked to puzzle the sheriff a little longer, but Mr. Bean was getting impatient, so he asked for a hammer, and when it was brought he took the plaster pie down from the plate rail and smashed it open. And there were the bills.

"Well, t'aint a football exactly."

The sheriff just stood there for a minute. He gave Freddy a long look, then he turned around and walked right out of the room and went into his office and locked the door.

Mr. Bean was one of the best people at not saying anything in the whole county. He didn't say anything all the way home. Once or twice, though, Freddy thought he made a noise behind his beard which might have been a chuckle. But you never could be sure.

Bill was in the barnyard, and when Mr. Bean had unharnessed Hank and gone in the house, he said: "Hey, Hank, come on; we're waiting for you."

"What goes on?" Freddy asked, and Hank said: "Oh, little game we been playin' while you been away. Want to come? Maybe you'd enjoy it. Or maybe you wouldn't—I dunno."

So Freddy went. A crowd of animals were gathered together in the upper pasture. The cows and the dogs were there, and Peter, the bear, and his cousin, Joseph, and Mac, the wildcat, and a number of others. As he watched, Mac broke away and dashed across the field, followed by Joseph and Robert. The wildcat was carrying something in his mouth.

"Not a football!" Freddy exclaimed.

"Yeah," said Hank. "Well, 'tain't a football exactly—just a lot of rags tied up so we can carry it in our mouths. There aren't enough animals for two full teams. But we've been having a lot of fun; Mrs. Wurzburger got two teeth knocked out yesterday."

"Golly," said Freddy, "there's one game I don't want to play in! All those horns and teeth and claws flying around!"

"We're pretty careful," said Bill. "We've made some extra rules, so I guess nobody'll get really killed. How'd you like to coach, if you won't play?"

But Freddy said no thanks and after watching a while he went back to the pig pen and got to work on the next issue of the Bean Home News.

Chapter 18

The next game with Tushville was to take place on the following Saturday. But on Wednesday the sheriff drove up to the farm. "Your trial's been put forward, Freddy," he said. "Judge says he can hear it this afternoon. You'll have to come with me."

"But I ought to go to school today," said Freddy. "I haven't been in quite a while. And I won't be able to play in Saturday's game, either."

"Too bad," said the sheriff. "But being tried for a crime is a pretty good excuse for staying out of school. Come along."

There was a big audience in the courtroom

that afternoon to see Freddy tried for robbery. Most of them knew Freddy and many of them were his friends, but the general opinion seemed to be that a robbery, even if committed with the best of intentions, is not something that can be passed over with just a talking to. And so when Freddy was led in, closely guarded by the sheriff and two troopers with pistols, there was very little applause.

Freddy had persuaded Old Whibley to act as his lawyer to defend him. "But this is the last time," he told Freddy. "I can't spend my life getting you out of trouble. If a person is a born fool, it is a waste of time helping him." For the owl had defended him once before when Mrs. Underdunk had had him arrested for—she claimed—having tried to bite her. Everyone agreed that Old Whibley had handled the case in a masterly manner, and he had certainly made a monkey out of Mr. Garble, who had conducted the prosecution.

The first witness called was Mr. Weezer, and he told how, as the result of that phone call, he had given the five thousand dollars to Freddy at 10 A.M. on October 15th. As he mentioned the sum his glasses fell off, and the sheriff picked them up and handed them to him.

"You are certain that the pig that you handed the five thousand dollars to was this prisoner?" Old Whibley asked.

"Yes, sir," said Mr. Weezer, who was groping for his glasses, which had again jumped off his nose. He put them on and looked at Freddy. "Yes, sir," he said. "It was that pig there, Freddy."

"How was he dressed?"

"Just as he is now," said the bank president. For Freddy wore the school clothes, two sets of which he had bought for Weedly and himself at the Busy Bee.

"And what did you say to him when you handed him the five thousand dollars?" asked the owl.

Again the glasses fell off. Mr. Weezer caught them this time, put them on, said: "I told him: 'Here is the five thousand dollars,' " and immediately caught them as they dropped off for the fourth time.

Judge Willey leaned forward. "How long have you worn glasses, Mr. Weezer?" he asked.

"About twenty-five years, your Honor."

"Unless you are attempting to amuse the court with a juggling act," said the judge testily, "I can only conclude that you are an amazingly slow learner. It seems to me that in a quarter of a century you could have worked out some way of keeping them on. In any case, we cannot have the trial interrupted by these continual bouncings and scrabblings. I suggest that you either hold them in place, or tie them on."

So Mr. Weezer held them on.

"Now, Mr. Weezer," said the owl, "it is a well known fact, is it not, that at the mention of any sum larger than ten dollars your glasses always fall off?"

Mr. Weezer said it was true.

"I will ask you," Old Whibley went on, "if it is not true that at the moment when you handed the money to the person who you claim is the prisoner here, and mentioned the amount, your glasses fell off?"

"I don't remember," said Mr. Weezer.

"Yet you remember mentioning five thousand dollars to this person?"

"Yes."

"And do you say that your glasses did *not* fall off?"

"I—well, of course they must have."

"Quite so," said Whibley. "Now, do you see well without your glasses?"

"I can hardly see at all without them."

"And yet you claim that although your glasses fell off at the very moment you handed this money to him, you recognized this pig as the person to whom you gave it. Is that so?"

"Well," said Mr. Weezer, "I—"

"Answer yes or no," snapped the owl.

"Well—yes, of course I did." Mr. Weezer took out the handkerchief with the initials and dollar signs on it and wiped the perspiration from his forehead.

Old Whibley looked up at the judge. "I submit, your Honor," he said, "that Mr. Weezer, for whom I have the greatest respect"—he bowed to the banker—"was mistaken. In the course of his business, which has exclusively to do with money, his glasses are, I suggest, as often in the air or on the floor, as on his nose. He cannot therefore rely greatly on his eyesight, and must be forced very often to guess at what he sees. I suggest that he guessed at the identity of the person to whom, in this case, he gave the money."

The judge shook his head. "I don't think you have proved your point."

"In connection with the evidence of a witness whom I am now about to call," said the owl, "I propose to carry my proof one step further. I will call Mr. Metacarpus, manager of that sterling emporium, the Busy Bee."

Mr. Metacarpus walked up to the witness box slowly with his hands behind his back, blowing out his big moustache from time to time, and bowing to right and left—"Good afternoon, madam. A lovely day, sir, but cool; topcoats one flight up"—as he did in the store when he greeted customers.

"Now, Mr. Metacarpus," said Whibley, "I will ask you to cast your mind back to the morning of October fifteenth. You opened the store at what hour?"

"Quarter to nine."

"Were you there all morning?"

"Yes, sir."

"And during that time did you see a pig in pants and a sweater and a cap in the store?"

"I did."

"Was it the same pig, in the same clothes, that you now see sitting there with the sheriff?"

"Yes, sir."

"You are rather near-sighted, are you not, Mr. Metacarpus?"

"I am not!" said the manager indignantly. As a matter of fact everyone in town knew that he was, but he was too vain to wear glasses.

"You are, then, absolutely certain?"

Mr. Metacarpus blew out his moustache. "Of course I'm certain. I remember the—the person perfectly. He had the same rather villainous expression, and he was acting in a very peculiar manner, walking around for upwards of two hours and fingering the articles for sale, and looking about furtively to see if anyone was watching him. It is quite easy for a person with my experience to spot the criminal type, and I had no doubt about him. I am not surprised to see him here." And he sucked his moustache into his mouth and blew it out with a plop.

Bang! went the judge's gavel. "The witness will keep his surprise to himself," he said. "Also, the court will appreciate it if he will keep his moustache under better control."

Old Whibley resumed. "You would say then that the prisoner was in your store continuously from nine until eleven on the morning in question?"

"Until after eleven," said Mr. Metacarpus.

"Did he buy anything?"

"No, sir. Just handled things and put them down. At least I hope he did. I watched care-

Bang! went the judge's gavel.

fully, and while I did not actually see him steal anything, I have no doubt that some small items found their way to his pocket."

Freddy forgot for a moment where he was, for it made him angry to hear Weedly accused of shoplifting. He started up. "Why that's not so! Weedly wouldn't—"

"Shut up!" snapped Whibley, and the judge banged with his gavel. "Another disturbance of this kind," he said peering severely at the pig, "and I will have you removed from the courtroom."

"Why, that's exactly what we want you to do, your Honor," said Old Whibley.

"Eh?" said the judge. "Ah, I see. I forgot for the moment that the prisoner was—er—well, a prisoner. Continue, then."

"There is nothing much to say, your honor," said the owl. "I submit that my client has a perfect alibi. Mr. Weezer claims that it was the prisoner who took the money from him at 10 A.M., pretending to have been sent for it by Mr. Bean. Mr. Metacarpus, on the other hand, asserts that from nine to eleven on the same morning the prisoner was under constant observation in the Busy Bee. Now this pig cannot have been in two places at the same time. Mr.

Weezer's identification of him is doubtful, since his glasses were falling off at the time. Mr. Metacarpus' identification of him extended over a considerable period of time, and is therefore reliable."

"If the court pleases," said Mr. Weezer, "why do we not ask the prisoner?"

"If the prisoner wishes to testify in his own behalf, he may do so," said the judge. "On the other hand, if he does not wish to take the stand the law does not compel him to."

"My client does not wish to testify," said Whibley.

"But your Honor," protested Mr. Weezer, "everyone knows that he took the money. He told a lot of people so."

"I object," said Whibley. "That is mere hearsay, and not admissible as evidence."

"Objection sustained," said the judge. "Quiet! Order in the court!" he shouted, for Freddy's frends had begun to applaud. "Prisoner," he said addressing Freddy, "the court pronounces you not guilty. But," he said severely, "don't for goodness' sake do it again!"

Chapter 19

Freddy found out later that it was Mrs. Church's influence with Judge Willey that had got his trial put forward. Having heard that one of the reasons why it had been set for February was that the judge had such a lot of Christmas shopping to do, she went to him and agreed to do all his shopping for him, even adding that she would pick out a small surprise present and give it to him herself. The judge always got a lot of presents for Christmas from people he had tried and found not guilty, but the thought of one more so delighted him, that he agreed to hold the trial right away.

It made him for a time the most popular person in Centerboro, because now Freddy could play in the Tushville game. Even Mr. Weezer was pleased. He was one of the first to congratulate Freddy on his acquittal. "I knew of course that you didn't intend to keep the money," he said, "but I had to testify against you for the sake of appearances. What would all the people say whose money the bank takes care of if I just let somebody walk off with five thousand dollars?" He caught his glasses neatly and went on. "They would say that I was not protecting their interests."

Freddy said of course he, as a banker, understood that, and that there were no hard feelings.

As for the Beans, they were so happy anyway that they had their money back, and that Mr. Doty's flight had made their great sacrifice unnecessary, that they welcomed Freddy with open arms. At least Mrs. Bean did. Mr. Bean didn't say anything for a few days. Then, on the morning of the football game, just as Freddy was climbing on his bicycle to leave for Centerboro, the farmer stopped him.

"Got just one thing to say to you," he said, and paused, puffing on his pipe so fiercely that Freddy expected any second to see his whiskers burst into flames. "You goin' to apologize for taking that money?"

Freddy looked unhappy. "Why—I'm going to say I'm sorry if it worried you," he said. "But I did what I thought was right. I can't apologize for that, can I?"

"No!" shouted Mr. Bean. "No, you can't! That's the answer I wanted!" He took the pipe out of his mouth and gave Freddy a whack on the back that nearly tumbled him over his bicycle.

"And I ain't going to apologize to you, either," the farmer went on, "because I did what I thought was right, too." He put his pipe back in his mouth. "Well, I guess that's that." He whacked Freddy again. "Now you go out there today and bust those Tushville rowdies into kindling wood." And then as Freddy started out of the gate: "Just a minute," he said. "Mrs. Bean—you know how women are— she's kind of curious about that alibi of yours. Maybe you'll tell her about it tonight." He shook his head. "That alibi!" he said, and the creaking sound that the animals always thought was a laugh came out through the whiskers.

Freddy hadn't wanted to ask if the Beans were coming to the game, but when he ran out with the others on to the field, there they were in the buggy. But this time they were right up in front of the crowd. "Golly, what a mob!" said Jason. The combined population of Centerboro and Tushville was probably not more than four thousand, but there was twice that number there. The bank and all the stores had closed so that everybody could come, and the sheriff had closed the jail. He had locked it and brought the prisoners along—it was the only time the jail had ever been locked. People were there from all over the state; Mr. Camphor was there, and Senator Blore had come up from Washington; and nearly everybody who wasn't sick in bed had come over from South Pharisee. And not only people. There were many out-of-town animals—particularly pigs, who had assembled to cheer on the distinguished member of their race. And of course all the Bean animals—even the mice, even the Webbs, and Randolph, the beetle, and his mother, and Homer the snake, all in the buggy with the Beans.

"Hey, Jason," said Henry James, "do you see what I see? There's a horse over there in the Tushville crowd with knee pads on."

"Gee whiz!" said Jason. "Do you suppose—?"

"I know what it is," said Freddy, "but I didn't

want to say anything to you until I was sure. That Tushville man, Canner—remember? I had a note from him this morning. He says they plan to bring some animals to play. Let's see what Mr. Finnerty says."

Mr. Finnerty was pretty upset. "You boys can't play against horses," he said. "We'll have to call the game off."

Freddy took him aside and talked to him a few minutes. At first the coach looked doubtful, but then he said: "Well, we can try it. Line up as usual, so they can't claim we broke the rules first. And then if it's necessary, we'll try it your way."

When the teams took their positions for the kick-off a murmur of surprise and protest went up from the crowd. The make-up of the home team was the same as last time, but six of the regular Tushville players had been replaced by strangers. Four of these were men, and two were horses. With Black Beard and Butcher playing, there were only four real schoolboys on the team.

The crowd had been taken by surprise, and before any real protest could be made Centerboro had kicked off. Black Beard got the ball, and then there was nothing to it. Behind the two horses he raced down the field straight through the home team, who merely scrambled to get out of the way. Even Freddy didn't care to block a horse. The first touchdown was scored in less than a minute, and one of the horses kicked the goal.

Then the crowd broke loose. While Tushville was cheering, Centerboro rushed out on the field, and I guess they would have chased the Tushvillers back home, horses and all, if a few of the more level-headed citizens hadn't got in front of them and held them back. It took some time before any single voice could be heard, but at last, by waving his arms and yelling over and over again in his tremendous voice: "Ladies and gentlemen! Ladies and gentlemen!" Mr. Gridley got their attention.

"You have come out here," he roared, "to witness a contest between two schools. Not a gladiatorial contest between hired fighters and wild beasts. I suggest that we call the game off, and all go quietly home."

"Tushville is ready to play," said the Tushville principal, Mr. Kurtz. "If Centerboro refuses, Tushville wins by default."

There was a lot more angry yelling at this, but the two coaches and the referee, and several prominent citizens had joined Mr. Gridley in front of the crowd, which presently calmed down and waited to see what would happen.

At first there was quite an argument. The Tushvillers insisted on their right to play the men and horses, who, Mr. Kurtz asserted, were regularly enrolled pupils in his school. The Centerboro officials said nothing doing: let the regular teams play a decent game, as all the other schools did. Take out these ringers, they said, and they'd even take out Freddy. But the Tushvillers refused.

Now of course Mr. Gridley could have ordered the Centerboro team to leave the field. But he didn't. It may have been because he knew that he would be pretty unpopular around town if he let Tushville get away with it, but I think it was because he was mad, and really at last wanted his team to win. So he said: "We have come out here to play Tushville, and we will wait until the Tushville team gets here. This aggregation of ruffians is not the Tushville team. If it does not put in an appearance before five o'clock, Centerboro will win by default."

Well of course the Tushvillers just laughed at this. And it was then that Mr. Gridley's eye

One of the horses kicked the goal.

fell on Freddy. "Miserable pig!" he said angrily. "You are the cause of all this. If I hadn't been persuaded to let you in the school, we'd have had none of this trouble."

"You wouldn't have had any team either," said the sheriff.

"I think we can play that team and beat them," said Freddy.

Mr. Gridley said he was crazy. But Freddy went up and talked to him for a few minutes in a low voice.

"I don't like it!" said the principal. "I don't like it at all!"

But then Mr. Finnerty added his arguments. And at last: "All right! All right!" said Mr. Gridley. "But just how do you propose—"

"Just a minute," said Freddy, and he and Mr. Finnerty went into a huddle. They called over the sheriff, who in turn called over some of the prisoners, and then Mr. Finnerty wrote some things on a piece of paper and handed it to Mr. Gridley. "Here's our line-up," he said.

Mr. Gridley was scowling angrily when he took it, but as he read his face lightened, and suddenly he laughed right out. Nobody had ever seen him do that before. Then he faced the crowd.

"Ladies and gentlemen," he shouted, "I heartily disapprove of the very lax admission requirements which the Tushville principal, Mr. Kurtz, has adopted for his school. However, in order that the game may go on, I have decided to adopt the same requirements. I have pleasure in announcing the admission of nine new pupils to the Centerboro school. Now let the game go on." And I regret to say that he put his chin forward and stuck out his tongue at Mr. Kurtz.

So the teams lined up. And a roar of delight and laughter went up from the Centerboro crowd when they saw their home players take their positions to receive the kick-off. At left end was Mac, the wildcat. At his usual position, left tackle, was Freddy, and next him in order, Mrs. Wiggins, Hank, Mrs. Wurzburger, and Bill, the goat, at left end. The sheriff had said that several of the prisoners were anxious to play, so Red Mike, Looey and Big Sam went in. The only real Centerboro players were Irving Hill at quarterback and Jason Brewer at fullback. This was the line-up.

```
Left end...........Mac (wildcat)
Left tackle.........Freddy (pig)
Left guard.........Mrs. Wiggins (cow)
```

Center. . . . . Hank (horse)
Right guard. . . . . .Mrs. Wurzburger (cow)
Right tackle. . . . . .Red Mike
Right end. . . . . Bill (goat)
Left half. . . . . .Looey
Right half. . . . . Big Sam
Fullback. . . . . .Jason Brewer
Quarterback. . . . . .Irving Hill

Mr. Finnerty had told Jason and Irving: "You boys better stay out of all of the plays. After you've passed the ball to Looey or Sam, keep out of the way. We don't want you to get hurt. I don't think you need to worry about winning the game."

The Tushville team was good and scared, but there was nothing they could do now but play. They kicked off to Red Mike. Of course Mike didn't know one end of a football from the other, but being a burglar in private life he was a fast runner and when Jason called to him to run and pointed out the Tushville goal posts, he ran towards them. With Mrs. Wiggins galloping along on one side of him and Mrs. Wurzburger on the other, the Tushville tacklers didn't dare to try for him. He went through with no opposition. And the score was now 7–7.

At the end of the quarter the score was 46–13, and Black Beard was out of the game. On one play he had got into the clear with the ball. He was running for a touchdown, and chasing along behind him were Bill and Mac. Mac would probably have been able to make a fairly good tackle if, in the excitable way of wildcats, he had not let out a screech before he leaped. But the sound of that terrible wildcat scream spurred Black Beard to just enough extra speed to forge ahead, and Mac missed. "Get him, Bill!" he yelled.

So Bill lowered his horns and dug in his toes. He caught Black Beard five yards from the goal line. But he couldn't tackle, he could only butt. So he butted. He hit Black Beard square in the middle of the seat of his football pants with a smack that you could have heard for half a mile. And Black Beard went the last five yards without touching the ground, and landed sitting down for a Tushville touchdown. But when he got up, he said: "I've had enough!" and he hobbled off home.

The second quarter was much the same. Mr. Finnerty had advised Hank and the cows not to do any hard blocking. "We don't want to kill those ringers," he said. "Just try to box them in so they can't tackle. With the horses use your own judgment. But I think they really just came out for fun, so take it easy."

So it was more of a dodging game than a game of blocking and tackling. And Centerboro was 104 to 13 at the end of the second quarter.

Strangely enough during the rest of the game nobody got hurt. That is, not badly enough to be carried off the field on a stretcher. Mac kept his claws in, but he snarled and spit with such ferocity that the runners he started for just lay down and covered their heads with their arms. The cows tried to be careful with their horns, and even though a fight or two started they didn't amount to much. Hank was the only one that got into what might have been a serious brawl.

There was a big bay horse on the Tushville team named Jock. Running down the field to intercept a pass, he fell over Mrs. Wiggins' hoof. I don't know whether she had put it out on purpose or not, but he went right down on his big Roman nose.

"Hey, you stupid idiot!" he said. "Keep your clumsy feet out of the way!"

"That ain't any way to speak to a lady," said Hank.

"Oh, yeah?" said Jock. "Want to make something of it?"

"Why, I dunno," said Hank in his slow way. "Dunno's I want to make any fuss, but—"

"Oh, you dunno!" Jock mimicked him. "Well make something of this!" And he put back his ears and snapped with his long teeth at Hank's shoulder.

Hank dodged. "Like I said," he went on calmly, "I don't want to create any disturbance, but I dunno—maybe it's better to create it and get it over with. It's going to hurt me worse than it hurts you though, because I got the rheumatism in my right hind leg." And suddenly he whirled right around, put his head down, and kicked out with both hind legs, and the heavy iron shoes went Whang! against Jock's ribs.

All the fight went out of Jock. "You big bully!" he said, and if a horse can look as if he was going to cry, he looked that way. And he trotted off.

The final score was 184–17. Freddy was surprised that Tushville didn't protest it. But he found out why after the excitement and cheering was over, and after the prisoners had smashed up the goal posts and begun to peddle the fragments around as souvenirs at five cents apiece. The Tushville people, so Mr. Finnerty had heard, were going to train a lot of heavy farm horses for the game, and by next year they could lick anything Centerboro could bring against them.

"We'll have to put a stop to that," said Freddy, and he went over to talk to Mr. Kurtz, who was walking grumpily off the field behind his team.

"Just a minute," Freddy said, and, when the Tushville principal turned angrily on him, he said: "I just want to tell you: Mr. Boom-schmidt, the circus man who comes through here every summer, is a friend of mine, and I am going to write and ask him to lend our team a couple of elephants and a lion, and maybe that rhinoceros, Jerry, for next year's game. I think," he said, "that we'll be able to give you some pretty good competition."

"Bah!" said Mr. Kurtz, and walked off. But that was the last anyone ever heard of the Tush-ville horses and the following year their team played straight football with the regular pupils, and both games were a tie.

Some days later a group of the animals were in the cow barn when Mrs. Bean brought a letter the mailman had left for Freddy. He read it slowly, and at the end looked up and said in a surprised tone: "What do you know! Why, his last name was easier to guess and commoner than his first name. It's Brown. Clarence Brown."

"Clarence?" said Charles. "You mean old Doty?"

"Yes. Look, he says here: 'I just want to tell you I'm sorry for all the trouble I gave those nice Bean people. I got a mean streak in me. I didn't really want to do them out of all their money, but I was hard up, and when Herb Garble wrote to me about it—'"

"Oh, fish feathers!" Jinx interrupted. "Sure, he's sorry, now he didn't get it. Sure, sure; so am I always sorry when I try to swipe something off the kitchen table and it don't come off."

"Well, I don't know," said Mrs. Wiggins. "He could really mean it. There were some nice things about him."

"That's true," said Freddy. "He tried to help me out several times. But he also tried to side-swipe me with his car one day, too. He and Garble were a pair. I hear Garble's left town for good."

"It's for *our* good," said Mrs. Wiggins. "But I kind of miss Doty, at that."

"So do I," said Freddy. "He was fun sometimes. And even when he wasn't, he made things plenty exciting. It does seem awfully quiet around here since he left. It would be nice to have a little excitement. Even my poetry seems sort of dull to me today."

"You and me too," said Jinx.

"I started one about the game," said Freddy without paying any attention to the cat's remark.

Black Beard, the Tush villain,
Came down to make a killin',
Came down with all his forces,
Big men and big horses;
Came down with Mr. Kurtz,
But Bill hit him where it hurts.
Black Beard, the Tush villain,
Had a wife and two chillun',
Brought 'em down to see the game,
Went back sore and lame;
Went back full of aches,
Didn't have what it takes;
Went back badly beaten;
Off the mantelpiece he's eatin'.
Black Beard, the Tush—

"Ho hum," said Jinx. "Guess I'll go hunt me up a little excitement."

Freddy looked up. Jinx was just going out of the door and otherwise, except for himself, the barn was empty.

"Darn it!" said Freddy. "Even when you write about *them,* they won't listen!"

A NOTE ON THE TYPE

The text of this book was set on the Linotype in Baskerville. Linotype Baskerville is a facsimile cutting from type cast from the original matrices of a face designed by John Baskerville. The original face was the forerunner of the "modern" group of type faces.

John Baskerville (1706-75), of Birmingham, England, a writing-master, with a special renown for cutting inscriptions in stone, began experimenting about 1750 with punch-cutting and making typographical material. It was not until 1757 that he published his first work. His types, at first criticized, in time were recognized as both distinct and elegant, and his types as well as his printing were greatly admired.